CW01080337

ABOUT THE AUTHOR

Barbara Cartland, the world's most famous romantic novel-
ist, who is also an historian, playwright, lecturer, pol'tical
speaker and television personality, has now written over 531
books and sold over 500 million copies all over the world.

She has also had many historical works published and has
written four autobiographies as well as the biographies of her
mother and that of her brother, Ronald Cartland, who was
the first Member of Parliament to be killed in the last war.
This book has a preface by Sir Winston Churchill and has just
been republished with an introduction by the late Sir Arthur
Bryant.

"Love at the Helm" a novel written with the help and
inspiration of the late Earl Mountbatten of Burma, Great
Uncle of His Royal Highness The Prince of Wales, is being
sold for the Mountbatten Memorial Trust.

She has broken the world record for the last sixteen years
by writing an average of twenty-three books a year. In the
Guinness Book of Records she is listed as the world's
top-selling author.

Miss Cartland in 1978 sang an Album of Love Songs with
the Royal Philharmonic orchestra.

In private life Barbara Cartland, who is a Dame of Grace of
the Order of St. John of Jerusalem, Chairman of the St. John
Council in Hertfordshire and Deputy President of the St.
John Ambulance Brigade, has fought for better conditions
and salaries for Midwives and Nurses.

She championed the cause for the Elderly in 1956 invoking
a Government Enquiry into the "Housing Conditions of Old
People".

In 1962 she had the Law of England changed so that Local
Authorities had to provide camps for their own Gypsies. This
has meant that since then thousands and thousands of Gypsy
children have been able to go to School which they had never
been able to do in the past, as their caravans were moved
every twenty-four hours by the Police.

There are now fourteen camps in Hertfordshire and Barbara Cartland has her own Romany Gypsy Camp called
Barbaraville by the Gypsies.

Her designs "Decorating with Love" are being sold all over
the U.S.A. and the National Home Fashions League made

her in 1981, "Woman of Achievement".

Barbara Cartland's book "Getting Older, Growing Younger" has been published in Great Britain and the U.S.A. and her fifth Cookery Book, "The Romance of Food" is now being used by the House of Commons.

In 1984 she received at Kennedy Airport, America's Bishop Wright Air Industry Award for her contribution to the development of aviation. In 1931 she and two R.A.F. Officers thought of, and carried the first aeroplane-towed glider air-mail.

During the War she was Chief Lady Welfare Officer in Bedfordshire looking after 20,000 Service men and women. She thought of having a pool of Wedding Dresses at the War Office so a Service Bride could hire a gown for the day.

She bought 1,000 secondhand gowns without coupons for the A.T.S., the W.A.A.F.s and the W.R.E.N.S. In 1945 Barbara Cartland received the Certificate of Merit from Eastern Command.

In 1964 Barbara Cartland founded the National Association for Health of which she is the President, as a front for all the Health Stores and for any product made as alternative medicine.

This has now a £650,000,000 turnover a year, with one third going in export.

In January 1988 she received "La Medaille de Vermeil de la Ville de Paris", (the Gold Medal of Paris). This is the highest award to be given by the City of Paris for ACHIEVE-MENT – 25 million books sold in France.

In March 1988 Barbara Cartland was asked by the Indian Government to open their Health Resort outside Delhi. This is almost the largest Health Resort in the world.

Barbara Cartland was made a Dame of the Order of the British Empire in the 1991 New Year's Honours List.

The Magic of Paris

Eva, beautiful, young and very innocent, finds herself alone in Paris.

Her father, the charming and distinguished Sir Richard Hillington, has died of a heart attack in the house of Leonide Leblanc, one of the most famous of the Courtesans in the Second Empire.

After the funeral, Eva finds that her father's shirt-stud – a pearl surrounded by sapphires – which had been given to him by her mother who is also dead, is lost.

Having no idea who Leonide Leblanc is, she goes to her house to ask her if there is any chance it fell off when he collapsed and died.

While she is seeing Leonide Leblanc, Lord Charles Craig comes to ask the advice of the most witty and clever woman in Paris.

He has been told privately that Raphael Bischoffheim who is the famous banker and who owes him money for the horses he has bought from him intends that he shall be his son-in-law.

Horrified at the idea which would undoubtedly scandalize his brother the Duke of Kincraig, Lord Charles begs Leonide Leblanc to save him.

She does so by persuading Eva for a large sum of money to pretend to be his fiancée, but makes her promise not to reveal her real identity.

Out of the twisted puzzle of deception and intrigue Eva is finally rescued from the intolerable advances of the *Marquis* by the Duke.

In doing so she finds a solution not only to Lord Charles' problem, but to her own.

BARBARA CARTLAND

The Magic of Paris

Mandarin

THE MAGIC OF PARIS

First published in Great Britain 1991
by Mandarin Paperbacks
Michelin House, 81 Fulham Road, London SW3 6RB

Mandarin is an imprint of the Octopus Publishing Group,
a division of Reed International Books Limited.

Copyright © Cartland Promotions 1991

A CIP catalogue record for this title
is available from the British Library
ISBN 0 7493 0838 9 PB
ISBN 0 7493 0945 8 HB

Printed in Great Britain
by St Edmundsbury Press Ltd, Bury St Edmunds, Suffolk

AUTHOR'S NOTE

On 2nd September 1870 the Emperor Napoleon III of France, surrendered to the Prussians at Sudan.

It was the end of the Monarchy and the beginning of the Third Republic.

The Second Empire, had been proclaimed on the 2nd December 1852, at the Hotel de Ville and the new Emperor rode into his Capital through the Arc de Triomphe.

The Second Empire was his creation and it was Louis Napoleon who moulded the social and political character of it.

For eighteen years France enjoyed a glittering, brilliant Imperial Regime.

The wild extravagance of the Courtesans, their jewels, their luxury and their arrogance astounded all Europe.

At the same time it all contributed to French History.

The ultimate disaster was partly the Empress Eugene's fault, who declared openly that their son would not reign unless the Emperor destroyed the military supremacy of Prussia.

It was she, combined with the Foreign Minister, the Duc de Gramond, who pressured the Emperor who was ill and suffering from acute pain as a result of a stone in his bladder into declaring war.

Bismarck, on the other hand knew the French Army was completely unprepared for modern warfare, whilst he had trained an enormous fully equipped Army.

The Royal Family escaped to Britain where the Emperor suffered two operations.

He seemed to survive them and the third had been arranged in 1873.

That morning while the doctor was with him the Emperor murmured:

"We were not cowards at Sudan."

They were his last words. He died before the operation could take place.

He had planned to return to France, hoping it would lead to his restoration on the throne.

The death of his son, the Prince Imperial, six years later, deprived not only the Bonapartes of any future, but France of a Monarchy.

CHAPTER ONE
1869

Eva looked helplessly round the room in which she was sitting.

It was a very attractive room, furnished with the exquisite inlaid and gilt furniture which only the French could design.

There was an Aubusson carpet on the floor.

The pictures while not by great artists, were French and very attractive.

When Eva had first seen the house she had exclaimed to her father:

"It is like an adorable dolls'-house! Oh, Papa, how lucky we are!"

"We are indeed!" Sir Richard Hillington replied.

He was thinking not only of the house, but also that he was in Paris again.

He had always loved Paris more than any capital City in the world.

When, six months ago, he had learnt that his wife had been left a house in Paris by her grandmother the *Comtesse* de Chabrillin he was elated.

Unfortunately, Lady Hillington had already contracted the disease which was to kill her very quickly.

Her husband always thought it was because they had visited the Alps.

9

He had bought her a fur coat and wrapped her up as warmly as he could.

But the treacherous winds from the snowy peaks had affected her lungs.

She had died four months after she learned that she owned the house in Paris.

It was said that she had not been strong enough to cross the Channel to see it.

Sir Richard Hillington adored his wife.

He had given up the prospect of early promotion in his Diplomatic career in order to marry her.

They had in fact run away.

He had been in Paris when he had met what he thought was the most beautiful girl he had ever seen.

She was engaged when she was very young, as was usual amongst the French aristocratic families.

The Bridegroom to be was a Frenchman a little older than she was and whose blood was as blue as hers.

The marriage had been arranged, and the gifts were already beginning to arrive.

Then Lisette de Chabrillin ran away with Richard Hillington.

It was the sort of thing, the French said, which might occur in England, but not in France.

Lisette's parents thought their daughter had behaved disgracefully.

How could she jilt a French nobleman to whom she was already betrothed?

They were also not impressed with the Englishman she had chosen in his place.

Lisette did not hear from her family for years.

In fact it was only when her father-in-law died.

Her husband then came into the title, and became the 5th Baronet.

After that, there was a somewhat cool communication between the Hillingtons and the Chabrillins.

But there was no invitation to visit France.

Lisette sometimes longed to see her family.

Actually she was completely content with the husband she adored, and their beautiful daughter who was very like herself.

Eva had inherited her mother's figure and large dark, eloquent eyes, but her father's fair hair.

It was a strange but compelling combination.

Sir Richard was well aware when she made her début that his daughter would become an acclaimed Beauty overnight

This should have been at the beginning of the year, but Eva was in deep mourning for her mother.

What was worse, her father had only just discovered that they were very short of money.

He had given up his Diplomatic career after his father died and had never reached the rank of Ambassador.

He had to cope with a large, unwieldy house in Gloucestershire.

The estate which required a great deal of money spent on it.

He had always thought his father was reasonably well off.

But the farms, which were let, had deteriorated over the years.

Sir Terence had apparently not been a good administrator.

Nor did he have any knowledge of finance.

He had invested in Companies which had gone bankrupt and lent money to friends who forgot to return it.

Sir Richard tried to save his home which had been in the family for two-hundred years.

It was an impossibility.

11

Finally, when his wife died, he realised that the only possible thing he could do was to sell the house in Gloucestershire.

He and Eva would then move to Paris.

There at least they would have a roof that did not leak over their heads.

Eva was delighted because it meant her father was happy.

He had been so miserable after his wife's death, that she thought he would never smile again.

She also knew it was impossible for him to go on living in the wilds of the country without decent horses.

He could not afford servants to run a big house.

Certainly he could not spend money on entertainment or hospitality.

"We will go to Paris, Papa," she said. "I am sure everything will be cheaper there."

Sir Richard was rather doubtful about this.

At the same time he knew that Gloucestershire was making him despondent.

Also it was also not the right place for his daughter.

He was well aware how beautiful she was.

He lay awake at night wondering how he could best present her to the Social World.

Only there would she meet the right sort of men she could marry.

He had no intention of forcing her into marriage.

He wanted her to be as happy as he had been with her mother, but without the scandal.

He had never counted the cost of marrying Lisette de Chabrillin because he was so ideally happy with her.

He knew however, that if he had not caused a scandal, he would have become an Ambassador.

12

The French had been very vehement in their denunciation of him.

Otherwise he would have been in a very much more important social position than he was now.

Nevertheless, no one could query the antecedents of the Hillingtons.

Yet he thought a little cynically they might be more appreciated in France than they were in England.

Eva was still suffering from the shock of her mother's death.

They had finished disposing of the house in Gloucestershire and everything they possessed.

Then she found that she and her father were as excited as two School-children going off on an adventure.

Eva had never been to Paris.

But Sir Richard had gone there once or twice since his marriage on his way to other Capitals in Europe.

His wife had not been with him.

She had however, talked to her daughter about the land to which she belonged.

She had made Paris seem a Fairy Tale City.

Eva arrived with her father late one evening.

When they had inspected the little house in the Rue St. Honore she knew her mother must have guided them there.

The house, which had belonged to her grandmother through her family and not the Chabrillins, was small but exquisite.

It had been built between two much larger houses

It was Eva thought, a part of her dreams, and she would wake up to find it had vanished.

The *Comtesse* had decorated every room as if it was a marvellous jewel.

Everything seemed to have been specially made or designed for the place in which she had put it.

The bedrooms with their canopied beds of silk and muslins were only fit, Eva thought, for Royalty.

"Now my dearest," her father had said, "we will enjoy together the most civilised and the most exciting City in the world."

He took her to dine at the *Café Anglais*.

It was, he told her, the smartest place in Paris.

It was patronised by everyone who was of any importance

It was certainly full, and a great many of the other diners remembered her father.

From that moment, Eva thought, he was swept away from her, so that she felt as if she had lost him.

He arranged for them to ride in the *Bois* and took her to see one or two of the traditional sights of Paris.

But after that, almost every evening he said:

"Will you forgive me, dearest, if I dine out tonight and leave you on your own?"

"But of course, Papa, but why cannot I come too?"

Sometimes the answer was that the party was for men only.

But often her father was far more evasive and said:

"It is a party at which your mother would not wish you to be present."

"Why not, Papa?" she queried.

"Because, my dear, the ladies, who I admit are very attractive, would not be accepted by your grandmother the *Comtesse* or, for that matter, by any of your Hillington relatives."

He did not say anything more about the friends to whom he went alone.

Eva was naturally very curious about them, and thought perhaps they were some of the ladies she had seen driving in the *Bois*.

They were certainly spectacular.

14

But the clothes they wore and their horses and carriages appeared to be more suited to the Theatre than to ordinary everyday life.

Then a week ago had come disaster.

It was so terrible that Eva could still not believe it had really happened.

Her father had sat with her while she ate her own dinner at the English hour of seven-thirty.

He had talked to her while she ate.

But he had already told her he was dining later with some of the mysterious friends who she was not allowed to meet.

She thought, as he sat with her in the small beautifully furnished Dining-Room, that he looked very elegant.

He had always seemed rather dashing.

Even though now he was nearing fifty he was still exceedingly handsome.

The few grey hairs appearing at his temples made him look more distinguished than he was already.

He still had a slim, athletic figure.

His evening clothes made in Savile Row fitted him without a wrinkle.

He was wearing, Eva noticed, on the front of his stiff shirt a single pearl surrounded by several small sapphires.

Her mother had given it to him for his birthday three years ago.

Lady Hillington had saved for a whole year to buy it.

It had delighted Sir Richard, not only because it was something he enjoyed wearing.

It was also an expression of his wife's unchanging love.

Eva could remember all too vividly how her father had opened his present, and stared at it incredulously.

He had then put his arms around his wife.

"Thank you very much, my darling," he said. "But how could you give me anything so delightful and so perfect that I can only thank you like this."

As he spoke he kissed her mother passionately.

Eva knew she was forgotten and tactfully crept away to leave them alone.

"You look very smart, Papa," she said as she put down her knife and fork.

"I am glad you think so," he replied, "because I am up against a lot of competition."

"Competition?" Eva enquired.

There was a twist to his lips as he said:

"The lady who is dining with me has already had a dozen other invitations!"

There was a sparkle in his eyes as he spoke.

Eva thought that he was excited at having defeated the other competitors, whoever they might be.

When her father left her she had picked up the book she was reading and gone up to bed.

She read until after midnight, then fell asleep.

She was wakened by the French man-servant who, with his wife, looked after them saying:

"Wake up, *M'mselle*! Wake up!"

Eva did so with a start.

"What is it?" she asked. "What has happened, Henri?"

"It's *Monsieur*, *M'selle*, he has been brought back, and he is ill, very ill!"

Eva scrambled out of bed and put on her dressing-gown.

Quickly she ran down the stairs to find her father had been carried into the house by two men dressed as coachmen.

They were standing in the Sitting-Room looking at him where he lay on a sofa.

Eva rushed to his side.

He looked as if he was asleep.

Yet at the same time there was something about the pallor of his face and the coldness of his hand.

When she touched it she was terrified.

She sent the coachmen for the Doctor.

By the time he came she knew before he confirmed it that her father was dead.

He had died of a heart-attack.

It was all the more poignant because Eva had never known there was anything wrong with him.

He had always seemed so strong, so well and, as he often said himself:

"I have not a pain in the whole of my body!"

Two days later he had been buried in the Cemetary of the British Embassy.

When the Service was over the British Ambassador, who was present, had said to Eva;

"I expect, my dear, you will want to return to England, and of course, I shall be only too willing to help you in any way I can."

"I thank Your Excellency," Eva answered.

"Well, you know where you can find me," the Ambassador said, "and I shall be expecting to hear from you."

She had come home alone.

Apart from the Ambassador whom she had never met before, she thought despairingly, there was no one she could consult about herself.

She was alone.

She supposed the Ambassador was right in thinking she should return to England.

There were a number of her father's family who she felt would offer to look after her.

But it would definitely be as a duty rather than something they wished to do.

17

She always had the feeling when she was with her father's relatives that they thought it rather odd of him to be so in love with her mother.

Although they had been very pleasant they were not really friendly to a foreigner.

Eva knew her mother had in return found them dull and dowdy.

"*Les Anglais*," she had exclaimed often enough to her small daughter, "have not the gaiety of the French They seem to take the sparkle out of the air, and even the sun shines less brightly when they come to see me."

"Why is that, Mama?" Eva had asked.

"Because the English are very, very serious, *ma petite*," Lisette Hillington replied. "They are too much concerned with things that are wrong, and not with those that are right."

She had laughed as she spoke.

But, on thinking over what she had said, Eva came to the conclusion that it was true.

Her father's relations nearly always started their sentences with:

"I am afraid this will distress you . . " or "I think you ought to know . . "

One of their favourites was:

"Of course, it is no business of mine, BUT . . "

"I am glad I am half-French, Mama," she had said to her mother.

Lady Hillington had laughed, and kissed her.

"So am I," she had replied, "but you are also your father's daughter, and I thank *le Bon Dieu* there is always a smile on his lips and a twinkle in his eyes."

"That was true," Eva thought.

Because her father had laughed when they had so little money she had laughed too.

"Something will turn up!" he said.

Then, when he saw the pretty little house in Paris, he exclaimed:

"How can we be so lucky as to have anything so lovely all to ourselves? It makes me feel as if your mother was with me because it is so like her."

Looking at the small Salon now, Eva knew exactly what he meant.

"I am here in Paris with Mama," she told herself, "and why should I return to England? Why should I live with Papa's relations in one of those dull, gloomy houses where the furniture is of dark mahogany and the curtains shut out the sun?"

She walked round the room looking at the pictures, the Louis XIV chairs, and a beautiful commode with its gilded handles and feet.

'I could sell some of this,' she thought, 'but instead I will work so that I can keep it just as it is.'

Even to take away one picture or one chair from any of the rooms would make her feel as if she was committing a crime.

She was however, practical enough to know that the small amount of money her father had transferred to the Bank would soon be spent.

Then there would be nothing to pay the servants' wages.

Besides there would be the inevitable question of food.

"But what can I do?" she asked herself.

It was then she remembered something she had not thought of since her father had died.

He had been taken upstairs and undressed before the Doctor arrived.

It was then that Henri the man-servant had noticed that the shirt-stud he had been wearing was missing.

It was the pearl and sapphire one which her mother had given him.

Eva thought when he had his heart attack it must have fallen from his shirt.

She had asked Henri if he knew with whom her father was dining.

She remembered how that he had said, as if he was reluctant to tell her:

"It was *Madame* Leonide Leblanc, *M'mselle*."

In her grief and while she was seeing to all the preparations for the Funeral, Eva had not thought of it again.

Now she decided she would call on *Madame* Leblanc.

She would ask her if she had found her father's shirt-stud.

It would give her something to do, and it was a mistake to sit in the house trying not to cry.

She put on her black bonnet.

Because she had bought it in Paris, it was a very becoming one.

She flung a silk shawl over her shoulders. As it was a warm day it was all she needed.

Her gown, although it was black, revealed the perfection of her figure.

She had never given it a thought, but it showed off the clarity of her skin which was very English.

Also the gold of her hair which she had inherited from her father.

As she came down the stairs she found Henri, who was a middle-aged man in the hall.

He and his wife, who was a little older than he was, ran the whole house.

"You're going out, *M'mselle*?" he enquired.

"Yes, Henri, and I want you to tell me the address of *Madame* Leonide Leblanc."

Henri looked at her in astonishment before he replied.

20

"Why should you want to know that, *M'mselle*?"

"I intend to call on her to ask her if she has found Papa's pearl shirt-stud. I feel sure it must have fallen off when he collapsed."

Henri looked worried.

"I'll do that for you, *M'mselle*," he said.

"There is no need, Henri," Eva replied. "Just let me have the address."

"It is in the *Rue d'Offemont* but it is not correct, *M'mselle* for you to go to the house of . . "

Henri paused for the right word, and Eva said:

"But I want to go and I think the lady, who was a great friend of my Father's, would like to see me."

Because Henri seemed incapable of it, she opened the front door herself.

Before he could say any more she had walked out into the street.

If she had looked back she would have seen he was looking after her with a worried expression in his eyes.

She had studied the map of the part of Paris where they were living and she realised that the *Rue d'Offemont* was not far.

It was a sunny day and she felt her spirits lifting above the grief and misery which had encompassed her since her father's death.

As she walked along she had no idea that almost every man who passed her turned to look back.

Nor that there was an expression of admiration in their eyes.

No Frenchman could resist a beautiful woman, and Eva was very lovely.

She reached the street and a *gendarme* told her which house it was.

She raised the very elaborate, highly polished knocker on the door.

It made a loud rat-tat.

The door was opened almost immediately by a servant dressed in what she thought was a very spectacular livery.

"Would it be possible," Eva asked in her perfect French, "for me to speak to *Madame* Leonide Leblanc:"

"I'll ask *Madame* if she's receiving," the servant replied. "Who shall I say is calling?"

"I am Miss Eva Hillington, daughter of the late Sir Richard Hillington."

The servant showed Eva into a room.

It was at the side of what she thought was the rather over-furnished hall.

The furniture was certainly valuable, but there was rather too much of it.

She thought too that the room was somewhat over-crowded and the curtains trimmed with too many tassels.

But what surprised her most were the flowers.

There were huge baskets, vases and bowls of them everywhere.

They were, she noticed, all the most exotic and expensive blooms.

There were orchids, tiger lilies, carnations and Parma violets which could only have come from a different part of France at this time of the year.

The servant reappeared.

"*Madame*'ll see you, *M'mselle* if you'll come upstairs."

The man went ahead and Eva followed him.

When she reached the landing he opened a door and she walked in.

To her surprise, she was in a bedroom, and *Madame* Leblanc was in bed.

It was not like any bedroom Eva had ever seen before.

Apart from the bed which was hung with blue silk curtains from a corolla of gold cupids, the whole place was full of orchids.

There were orchids on tables, and huge vases of them on the floor

It made the place a bower for the striking appearance of its owner.

Leonide Leblanc was much younger than Eva expected.

She was not beautiful, nor even lovely.

But she had a fascinating face. Eva thought it would be very hard to forget her.

Her dark hair fell over her shoulders, and a lace nightgown barely concealed two perfectly rounded and rose pointed breasts.

She held out her hand on which there were several glittering rings and said:

"I am so desperately sorry about your dear father! It must have been a terrible shock for you!"

"It . . it was," Eva replied.

"He was a charming man," Leonide Leblanc went on, "and it would be difficult for a woman to refuse him anything!"

"I know that the night he died, he was delighted with the idea of dining with you, *Madame*."

"I have never known him in such good spirits," *Madame* Leblanc said. "But do sit down."

She pointed to a chair near the bed and, as Eva sat on it, she said:

"*Alors*, but you are very lovely, and that is what I would expect of your father's daughter."

"Thank you," Eva said, "but it will . . never be the same . . without him."

"That I understand," *Madame* Leblanc replied, "but you must be brave. What are you going to do with yourself?"

"Perhaps that is . . something I could . . ask you," Eva said.

"Ask me?"

The idea obviously astonished Leonide Leblanc.

"What I really came for, Madame," Eva said, "was to ask you if you have found my father's shirt-stud. It was a pearl surrounded by several small sapphires, which my mother gave to him."

Madame Leblanc gave a little cry.

"So that is who it belonged to! I wondered who could be the owner when it was found under the bed."

Eva's eyes widened for a moment.

Then she told herself that *Madame* Leblanc had obviously received her father as she was receiving her.

Perhaps he had sat on the very chair on which she was sitting now.

"I will return the stud to you," *Madame* Leblanc said. "In the meantime, tell me what you meant by saying that perhaps I could help you."

She sounded so friendly that Eva bent forward to say:

"I do not know whether or not Papa told you, but we have inherited a little house in the *Rue St. Honoré*. It is so pretty and so charming that I cannot bear to think of leaving it and going back to England as the Ambassador advised me to do."

"You want to stay in Paris?" Leonide Leblanc asked.

"I am half-French," Eva said, "and I know I would be happier here than in England with Papa's relations."

Madame Leblanc smiled as if she could understand that, and Eva continued:

"I have been wondering what I could do, and perhaps you could advise me. If I could find a position, perhaps teaching children, or doing anything, I could stay where I am, and earn enough money to afford it."

24

Madame Leblanc stared at her.

"Are you saying that your father has not left you any money?"

"Very, very little," Eva replied, "and what there is will not last for long."

"Then I must think," *Madame* Leblanc said.

She was looking at her, Eva thought, in a strange way, almost as if she was appraising her.

She could not help wondering if her appearance was an asset.

It might prove to be the opposite.

Eva was too intelligent not to realise that if she worked for a Lady as a Governess she might be considered too pretty.

Her employer might be jealous of her.

She looked at Leonide Leblanc anxiously.

She was thinking she had never seen anyone who managed to look so fascinating, even though she was in bed and her hair not arranged.

It was then that there was a knock on the door.

"*Entrez!*" *Madame* Leblanc said.

It was the man-servant who had let Eva in and he held in his hand a small gold salver on which lay a card.

Leonide Leblanc read it, then she said:

"Escort *Mademoiselle* Hillington to the Salon, and tell Chef to provide her with English tea. Then bring Lord Charles upstairs."

She said all this very quickly to the man-servant, in what was almost an aside.

Then she said to Eva:

"Listen my dear, I want to continue our conversation and to think how I can help you, but I have an important visitor whom I cannot refuse."

"I understand," Eva said, "and of course I could go and come back another day."

"No, no, that would be a mistake," Leonide Leblanc replied. "Go downstairs and wait until I can see you again. I sometimes have English visitors, so my Chef knows exactly what they always desire at four o'clock!"

She laughed, and because her laughter was so infectious, Eva laughed too.

"Now, run along," Leonide Leblanc said, "and I will not be longer than I can help."

Eva obeyed her, and followed the servant downstairs.

They crossed the hall into a different room from where she had been before.

It was larger and again there seemed to be too much furniture and too many flowers.

Here they were almost overwhelming.

Eva remembered that when she had passed through the hall there had been a number of baskets of orchids and lilies standing just inside the front door.

They had not been there when she first arrived.

"I think *Madame* Leblanc must be an actress," she told herself. "That is why she has so many bouquets, and she must be a very famous one!"

She seated herself on a velvet-covered sofa.

As she did so she wished she had been more inquisitive and made her father tell her more about his friends.

One thing was obvious! *Madame* Leonide Leblanc was very different from anyone she had met before.

Yet she could not help being somewhat shocked.

Madame was receiving her next visitor, who was called Lord Charles, in her bedroom.

CHAPTER TWO

When Eva had left the room Leonide Leblanc got out of bed and went to the dressing-table.

She powdered her nose, touched her lips with salve and sprayed herself with an exotic perfume.

It had been made specially for her.

Then she got back into bed and waited for Lord Charles to be brought upstairs.

Although Eva had no idea of it, Leonide Leblanc was one of *La Garde*.

They were the twelve most famous Courtesans in Paris.

While she was still young, she had already gained the name of '*Madame Maximum*'.

No one was quite certain whether it was due to her fees, her accoutrements or her extravagance.

More likely than anything else it was the number of her lovers.

Leonide had come to Paris with her father when she was five.

He was a shoe-maker in Burly, a small hamlet in the Loire *Département*.

He decided to take his daughter to Paris.

As they had no other means of travel, they had walked there.

A heavy shower of rain just before they reached the Capital of France had made Leonide's shoes unwearable.

She had therefore entered Paris bare-footed.

Her father who was ambitious, wished her to become a Governess and sent her to School.

There she was so clever that she won a number of prizes.

Her intelligence was acclaimed by the teachers.

Leonide, however, had no intention of being anything but an actress.

At fourteen, she ran away and got herself a part on the stage of the *Belleville Theatre* which was on the outskirts of Paris.

From there she moved to the *Théâtre des Variétés* where she was a great success.

But her fascination for men soon made it unnecessary for her to be an actress.

As she was to be described later:

> *"She was not only very witty, very intelligent, and very ambitious, she was also voluptuousness itself, in flesh and blood."*

Leonide's ambition made her bring *La galanterie* up to a fine art, and she soon had the most distinguished lovers in Paris.

Her most important was Henri d'Orleans, Duc d'Aumale.

The Grand Seigneur of Chantilly provided her with the most exquisite furniture and objets d'art that were the envy of everyone who saw them.

Leonide soon became not only one of the sights of Paris, but at Baden-Baden and Homburg.

At the latter, she won half-a-million *francs*.

'*La Vie Parisienne*' and the other magazines and newspapers of France, seldom went to press without mentioning her.

When she was twenty-six she was recognised as the most fascinating woman in the whole of the country.

Now, as she lay back against her pillows, she was thinking of Eva.

She wondered what she could do for Sir Richard Hillington's daughter.

She had found him charming, attractive and she enjoyed being with him without being paid for her favours.

She felt, because he had his fatal attack in her arms that she owed his daughter something.

Although what she could do for the girl she had no idea.

The door opened and Lord Charles came in.

The brother of the Duke of Kincraig, he was an extremely handsome young man with an infectious *joie de vivre* which made him popular wherever he went.

He had pursued Leonide relentlessly every time he was in Paris.

Finally she had succumbed to his importuning.

Even though he was in no position to give her the money or presents which her other lovers lavished on her.

She liked him because he was an aristocrat.

She found him very accomplished in bed and very amusing out of it.

He burst into the room now, walked across to Leonide, put his arms round her, and kissed her.

Then he sat down on the bed and said:

"*Ma Belle*, I am in trouble!"

"Not again!"

"This is worse than usual."

"How?"

"Because, my adorable Siren, I cannot see a way out unless you can think of one."

29

"Then I will try, Charles," Leonide said, "although I have no intention of paying your debts."

"It is not my debts," Lord Charles replied, "but it is a millstone round my neck, and fetters that I cannot remove from my legs."

Leonide settled herself more comfortably against her pillows.

"Now, start from the beginning," she said, "so that I can understand what you are saying."

She was speaking French.

Lord Charles was speaking in the same language, with a decided British accent.

At the same time, he was surprisingly fluent, and he began:

"When I was here a month ago the Millionaire Banker Raphael Bischoffheim asked me to find him some horses."

Leonide gave a little cry.

"I had heard that Bischoffheim had started a racing stable" she said, "and of course, English horses have so far done very well in France."

"That is why he asked me to buy him six or eight outstanding animals," Lord Charles replied, "and from the top owners in England."

"And you obliged?"

"They are arriving tomorrow."

"Then – what is wrong?" Leonide asked. "I am quite sure you will make Bischoffheim 'pay through the nose' for them!"

"That is what I intend he shall do," Lord Charles said, "although actually, because they are the most superb animals you will ever have seen, he will be getting a bargain however much he pays for them!"

"I believe you," Leonide smiled, "although a lot of people would not!"

30

"I arrived, as you know, yesterday," Lord Charles went on, "and came to see you; then, before I visited Bischoffheim, I went to the Club to hear the latest gossip."

"I am sure that was most informative," Leonide remarked a little sarcastically.

Lord Charles drew in his breath.

"I was told by a friend of mine that Bischoffheim, while looking forward to owning the horses, has also decided I would make an excellent husband for his eldest daughter!"

Leonide stared at him.

"I cannot believe that is true!"

"I can," Lord Charles replied. "The ambitious Banker not only intends to set up one of the best racing stables in France, but he also wishes to shine in England."

There was silence. Then Leonide said:

"It seems incredible, absolutely incredible! But what can you do?"

"That is what I came to ask you," Lord Charles replied.

He thought for a minute. Then he added:

"You can imagine what my brother would say if I suggested bringing Bischoffheim's daughter into the family. Besides, as you are well aware, I have no desire to marry anyone!"

"Do you really think," Leonide asked after a pause, "that if you refuse to do as he wishes, he will tell you to take your horses back to England?"

"I am fairly certain that is exactly what he plans. He knows I am heavily in debt, which is nothing new: he knows I have bought these horses on credit, and quite frankly, Leonide, I am in a tight corner with not the slightest notion of how to get out of it!"

"But you have to!" Leonide cried.

31

She looked at the handsome young man sitting opposite her, with his fair hair, blue eyes and clear complexion.

Then she saw Raphael Bischoffheim.

He was small, dark, a large nose, and a dazzlingly brilliant brain, but absolutely no breeding.

The aristocrats with whom Leonide associated, both French and English, had made it clear to her how much breeding mattered to them.

She was aware that Lord Charles was in what he had said himself, a 'very tight corner'.

"Come on," he was saying, "you have the reputation of being the cleverest woman in France. For God's sake, Leonide, save me! Think of what I can do, and what I can say."

"Bischoffheim is a hard man," Leonide said slowly. "If he has set his heart on marrying his daughter to an aristocrat, I will wager every *franc* I possess that somehow he will do it!"

"But not to me!" Lord Charles replied. "I am damned if I will marry a French girl who has nothing to offer except her father's money."

"You could do with it!" Leonide remarked.

"Not at the price of my freedom, and frankly, I would not soil the Family Tree with the name of Bischoffheim!"

"That is something you cannot say to him!" Leonide remarked.

"That is what I will have to say if he presses me, and what is more I will then have to take the horses back to England."

Lord Charles got off the bed and walked restlessly across the bedroom and back again.

"I had to go on my knees to get the horses I wanted," he said. "I even bought one from the Royal Stud!"

There was silence. Then he said:

32

"For God's sake, Leonide, tell me what I am to do! What *can* I do?"

There was another silence, then Leonide gave a little cry.

"I have it!" she said. "I have the perfect solution!"

Lord Charles went back to the bed to sit where he had sat before.

"What is it?" he asked.

"You must tell Raphael Bischoffheim before he tells you what he desires, that you are engaged to be married!"

"Engaged to be married?" Lord Charles asked. "But to whom? He is unlikely to believe that I have a *fiancée* in England if it has not been announced in *'The Gazette'!*"

"You will produce your *fiancée*," Leonide said slowly, "here in Paris!"

Lord Charles stared at her. Then he said.

"Leonide, you are a genius! But you will have to produce the girl, and she will have to look the part. Bischoffheim is no fool!"

"I am aware of that," Leonide replied, "and what you are saying is that she must be a Lady, and look like a Lady."

She saw the look in Lord Charles' eyes and added:

"It is all right. She will know she is acting a part, and you do not really wish to marry her, but you will have to pay her."

"I would give her the Crown Jewels, if she will get me out of this mess!" Lord Charles said impulsively.

"Be careful," Leonide said. "You have to make a profit on the deal."

Lord Charles laughed.

"Leonide, I adore you! Tell me exactly what you have planned."

33

Leonide hesitated, and he thought she was choosing her words.

"I know of a girl," she began, "who is definitely a Lady, but needs money so that she can stay in Paris."

"If she is good looking, I should not think there as any difficulty about what she can do!" Lord Charles said.

"I have told you she is a Lady," Leonide said sharply, "and if you are going to treat her as a *jolie poule* you can find your own solution to the problem."

Lord Charles flung up his hands.

"I am sorry, I apologise! Go on, I am listening."

"I will produce her," Leonide said, "on one condition and one condition only."

"What is that?"

"That you do not touch her, you do not try to make love to her, and you leave her exactly as you find her: a very pure and very innocent young girl."

Lord Charles stared at her.

"And you are going to produce her for me? Come on, Leonide, as you know, I adore you, but that does not sound as if she is likely to be a friend of yours or entrusted to you by her parents as a counsellor."

"That is my business!" Leonide said. "Do you, or do you not promise what I have asked you?"

"I promise! Cross my heart, and on the word of a gentleman!"

"Very well, this is what you must do."

She was obviously thinking out the programme ahead of him and Lord Charles waited in silence.

He was thinking as he looked at Leonide that there was no other Courtesan who could manage to be a friend to her lovers.

Nor was there one to whom he could have gone for help.

Leonide was different, and he was well aware that

to some of her lovers she talked Politics and to others Art.

Quite a number of men visited her whenever they came to Paris, just because they admired and liked her.

After he had waited for some time, Leonide asked:

"When are you getting in touch with Bischoffheim?"

"He has asked me to luncheon tomorrow, and I planned that afterwards we would go straight to his stables where the horses would have been delivered during the morning."

"Good!" Leonide exclaimed. "Now, what you have to do is to write him a note saying how much you are looking forward to seeing him, and to showing him what you have purchased on his behalf."

At the thought of the horses Lord Charles's lips tightened, but he did not interrupt.

"Then you will add that you are bringing with you someone you are anxious for him to meet."

"I do not say who it is?" Lord Charles questioned.

"No, not if the person is male or female. When you arrive you introduce her, at the same time swearing Bischoffheim to secrecy because your engagement has not been officially announced since your *fiancée* who is half-French, has not yet met your brother."

"It sounds too good to be true," Lord Charles said. "The only thing is – what is she like?"

"She will look the part, she will act the part, and you will keep your promise to me," Leonide said.

"All right," Lord Charles agreed. "At the same time, you had better fill in the gaps."

"I will do that tomorrow, when you collect her here at twelve noon," Leonide replied. "Now we have to decide how much you will pay her."

"What she gets will entirely depend on whether

35

Bischoffheim coughs up, but at the moment my pockets are 'To Let'!" Lord Charles said.

"That is what I expected," Leonide replied. "And because there will be no reason for him not to buy the horses after he has asked you to procure them for him, you will receive a cheque. I think my little *protégée* should receive – now, let me think . ."

"For God's sake, Leonide!" Lord Charles exclaimed "Leave me a few *francs* with which to enjoy myself. I might even buy you some orchids, as you seem so short of them!"

He was speaking facetiously, but Leonide paid no attention.

She was in fact calculating *francs* into pounds.

"I propose £500," she said.

Because Lord Charles had been frightened that it might be more, he held out his hand.

"Done!" he said, "but if she is not perfect in her part and Bischoffheim 'puts the boot in', she gets nothing!"

"Agreed!" Leonide said, and put her hand in his.

His fingers tightened and he kissed it, then bending forward he said:

"As usual, I find you irresistible!"

. . . .

Downstairs, Eva began to think that *Madame* Leblanc had forgotten her very existence.

She had eaten a large tea, in fact the *pâtisserie* were so delicious that she had been greedy and eaten two.

Then she inspected the Salon.

She found there was a collection of snuff-boxes that she was sure her father must have admired.

They were ornamented with diamonds, pearls and other precious stones.

Some of them also contained miniatures of the French Kings.

There was a beautiful collection of pink *Sèvres* on the mantelpiece which was very rare.

There were ornaments in jade and pink quartz which she was sure were extremely valuable.

Even while she was admiring such a wonderful collection of treasures she kept wondering what she should do.

How would it be possible for her to earn some money?

Perhaps if *Madame* Leblanc was on the stage she could find her a small part in the Theatre.

She was quite certain, however, that her mother would have been horrified at the idea.

"Why did I not discuss it with Papa before he died?" she asked herself.

She knew that if she had done so her father would merely have said in his happy-go-lucky way that 'something would turn up'.

She tried not to think that his Funeral had cost her a great deal, and that food in France seemed far more expensive than in England.

Of course at home they had had their own chickens and ducks.

In the winter, her father had shot the birds in the woods.

While the goods they had bought in the village shop had not seemed as expensive as those which Marie, who was Henri's wife, bought in the market.

"There must be something I can do!" Eva said to herself despairingly.

They were the same words that had echoed in her mind last night and the night before.

She was wondering whether she should go into the hall and ask if *Madame* Leblanc had really forgotten her.

Then a servant appeared and she was told she could go upstairs again.

She thought that *Madame*'s visitor, Lord Charles, had certainly been very long-winded.

However she hoped that *Madame* Leblanc had had time to think of her as well as of him.

She entered the bedroom and thought as she had before how attractive its owner looked.

There was a faint flush on her cheeks and her eyes seemed to be shining.

Although it might have been the sunshine coming through the windows.

"I am sorry to have been so long, *Ma cherie*," *Madame* Leblanc said, "but I know you will excuse me for having kept you waiting when I tell you that I have found employment for you."

Eva clasped her hands together.

"You have? How very, very kind of you! I have been praying that you would somehow find a solution to my problems."

Leonide Leblanc smiled a little wryly.

"I seem to have had quite a number of problems today," she said. "But I have solved yours, at least for the moment. Now sit down and let me tell you what you have to do."

Eva obeyed her and *Madame* Leblanc took a sip of what looked surprisingly like champagne, from a glass that was standing on a table by her bed.

Then Eva thought she must be mistaken.

She could not imagine anyone would drink champagne in bed.

At home her father and mother would occasionally open a bottle to celebrate a birthday or an anniversary and of course, at Christmas.

At other times it had been too expensive.

Then her father drank claret or white wine, while her mother preferred lemonade.

Leonide Leblanc took another sip. Then she said:

"Now, what you have to do is to act a part."

Eva gave a little cry.

"I was thinking," she said, "that because you must be on the stage and a very, very clever actress, that perhaps you could find room for me in the Theatre."

"It is not in the Theatre," Leonide replied sharply, "and as your father's daughter, I would not think of sending you on the stage."

Eva looked at her wide-eyed.

Then she flushed and said:

"I know Mama would not have . . approved . . but . . I thought perhaps it was the . . only thing I could . . do."

"It is something you should not do!" Leonide said, "and when I said 'act a part', this is something for which you are very well qualified."

Eva looked at her enquiringly, and *Madame* Leblanc went on:

"My last visitor, who has just left, was Lord Charles Craig, and he is in a difficult situation."

Eva had now heard his surname for the first time.

Although it sounded somewhat familiar, she did not remember any of her father's friends having the name of Craig.

"Lord Charles," Leonide Leblanc continued, "is a charming young man who has never been married and has *no wish to be*."

She spoke slowly, accentuating the last four words as if she wished to impress them upon Eva.

"He has, however," she went on, "become involved in an unfortunate situation through no fault of his own."

"What is it?" Eva asked.

"I do not suppose you have heard of the most influential Banker in Paris whose name is Raphael Bischoffheim?"

Eva shook her head.

"He has decided, and no one could afford it better, to have race horses which will outrun and beat those belonging to the members of the Jockey Club."

Eva smiled.

She could understand his ambition.

Her father had told her about the Jockey Club and how important its members were.

"*Monsieur* Bischoffheim asked Lord Charles to procure for him a number of horses from England, from the very best stables."

Leonide Leblanc threw out her hands as she finished and laughed.

"Now Lord Charles has found an obstacle that he had not foreseen."

"An obstacle?" Eva asked.

"*Monsieur* Bischoffheim wants Lord Charles to marry his daughter!"

Eva looked surprised.

"But . . surely . . ?" she began.

"Exactly!" Leonide Leblanc replied. "It is impossible for Lord Charles to marry *Monsieur* Bischoffheim's girl, however attractive she might be. And his brother, the Duke of Kincraig, would be furious at the idea!"

"I can understand that," Eva said.

She was wondering as she spoke how she came into the story.

"There is only one way," Leonide Leblanc went on, "by which Lord Charles can obtain the money he has expended on the horses, without offending *Monsieur* Bischoffheim by refusing to become his son-in-law."

Eva did not have to ask the question which trembled on her lips.

Leonide Leblanc added dramatically:

"If Lord Charles produces a *fiancée*!"

"Oh!" Eva exclaimed. "Then he is already engaged to be married!"

"I have already said that he has no intention of marrying anyone!" Leonide Leblanc replied.

"Then . . how . . how . . can he . . ?"

"Do not be stupid," Leonide Leblanc said. "Lord Charles will produce *you* as his *fiancée*!"

"Me?"

"You have to pretend that you are the girl to whom he is engaged to be married!"

She paused a moment and then continued:

"When Lord Charles receives the cheque for the horses, which will amount to quite a considerable sum, you will discreetly disappear."

Eva looked bewildered.

"B . but . . suppose . . ?" she began.

"It is quite an easy thing for you to do," Leonide Leblanc said sharply. "You just have to be yourself, but you will of course have a different name, and even Lord Charles must not be aware of your real identity."

"Why not?" Eva asked.

"Because, my dear, it would embarrass him. Besides, if it was known in England that you had pretended to be engaged to a very distinguished young man, it would ruin your reputation, and certainly your chances of marrying the type of man your father would wish you to marry."

"Yes . . of course . . I understand," Eva said nervously. "Then . . who am I to . . be?"

Leonide Leblanc smiled.

"What is more important, and what you should be asking is how much is he going to pay you for doing this."

"But . . surely . . I do not . . have to . . ask him?" Eva said quickly. "I . . I would find that . . very embarrassing!"

"Of course you would! And that is why I have arranged it all for you. If you act your part convincingly and *Monsieur* Bischoffheim gives up his ridiculous idea of Lord Charles marrying his daughter, you will receive £500!"

Eva gave a gasp.

She knew that the average Governess in England received about forty pounds a year!

If she was careful £500 would enable her to let in her little house for quite a long time without worrying about money.

Because she was so surprised she said the first thing that came into her head.

"It . . it is . . too much!"

Leonide Leblanc laughed and held up her hands.

"Never refuse money, *ma Cherie*! Never say any sum is too much when you have to work for it, and in this case accept with gratitude what the gods are giving you."

"I think really I should be . . thanking you," Eva said. "How can you be so kind to me? I am so very . . very . . grateful!"

"I was fond of your father," Leonide Leblanc replied, "and I am repaying him for many hours of happiness we spent together."

"Then I am sure Papa . . wherever he is now . . is also very grateful to you," Eva said in a soft voice.

There was a little silence.

Then, as if Leonide Leblanc was afraid of becoming sentimental, she said:

"Now, let us get to work. I presume you have some clothes that *Monsieur* Bischoffheim will think suited a young English Lady, engaged to the brother of the Duke of Kincraig?"

"They are . . not very smart, I am afraid," Eva said apologetically, "but I have some of my mother's gowns with me which I can wear, but of course . . they are not black."

"You are not to wear black!" Leonide Leblanc exclaimed in horror. "You have to look happy, and who would not be happy if they were marrying Lord Charles?"

She thought for a moment. Then she said:

"I will send my maid back with you to your house and she can iron and tidy up what you have and perhaps add a ribbon trimming or lace to a gown if it looks too dull."

"That would be . . very kind," Eva said.

"And now we have to decide what you will call yourself."

"My name is Eva."

"That would be suitable as you have an English mother and a French father."

Eva laughed.

"The reverse is the truth."

"Of course, but you have to explain why you are in France, and not in England."

"And what is to be my French name?"

It flashed through Eva's mind that she might call herself 'Chabrillin' which had been her mother's name before she married.

Then she thought that might be dangerous in case *Monsieur* Bischoffheim knew any of the family.

"You will be Venarde," Leonide Leblanc decided. "'Eva Venarde'. It is very attractive, and you will not wish to talk a great deal about your family, so *Monsieur* Bischoffheim will not know."

"It would be embarrassing if he . . asked questions," Eva said.

"Then you must just be clever enough to speak gaily about something else."

"I will . . try . . I will try to do everything you tell me," Eva said humbly.

As she spoke she knew that her heart was singing.

£500 would mean that she could stay in Paris!

She could live in her own exquisite little house, and for the moment she was not afraid of the future.

Then as if Leonide Leblanc was looking at her for the first time, she said:

"You are very lovely! In fact beautiful, so perhaps I could give you a little advice, which I hope you will follow."

"You know I will do anything you say," Eva said. "I am so very grateful for your kindness to me."

"You can keep your thanks until the £500 is in your hand, and Lord Charles can leave Paris a free man."

"I am only . . afraid I shall . . make a mistake," Eva said.

"Why should you?" Leonide Leblanc asked. "You just have to be yourself, but remember, you are a very correct, prim and proper little English girl and you are embarrassed by fulsome compliments."

She paused for a moment before she said:

"And you quite understand – you do not allow any man to touch you."

"Touch me?" Eva exclaimed in surprise. "You mean . . they must not hold my hand?"

"I mean they must not kiss you!"

"I cannot imagine anyone would want to do that unless they knew me well," Eva said.

"No, of course not, and they would not have the opportunity if your mother was there to chaperon you."

Eva looked at her with frightened eyes.

"I . . I did not think of that . . and surely . . *Monsieur* Bischoffheim and Lord Charles would think it . . strange of me to be staying alone in my house in the Rue St. Honoré without a chaperon?"

"That is just what I was going to say to you," Leonide Leblanc said. "You must never reveal to either of them exactly where you are staying, or that you are living alone."

Eva's eyes widened and she went on:

"You are intelligent enough to say convincingly that you have your Aunt with you, but she is at the moment in bed with a bad cold and therefore cannot receive visitors."

She paused before she added:

"Neither can you, so if any man suggests coming to your house, you explain very politely that it would not be correct as your Aunt is ill."

"Yes, of course . . I understand," Eva said, "and it was very stupid of me not to think of that before."

She thought as she spoke that it was something of which in future she should certainly be careful.

She could not however imagine she would meet many men who would indicate that they would wish to call on her.

If they did, that was the answer.

Leonide Leblanc took another sip from her glass.

Then she said:

"I will ring for my maid Josie and tell her what I wish her to do, and also give you your father's shirt-stud."

She rang the bell by her bed as she spoke.

A few seconds later the door opened.

A maid dressed in black with a tiny lace-trimmed apron came into the room.

She was not young, in fact she was a woman of nearly forty.

She looked at Eva in what seemed to be a surprised fashion.

"This, Josie," Leonide Leblanc said, "is the daughter of Sir Richard Hillington, whom you will remember was taken ill here a week ago."

"Yes, indeed, *Madame* the poor gentleman! I was so sorry for him."

"Well, apparently it was his shirt-stud we found later," Leonide Leblanc said. "I want you to give it to Miss Hillington, and also, Josie, to go back to her house with her, to look at her clothes."

Now the maid was definitely surprised, and Leonide Leblanc said:

"I have set Miss Hillington a little task which will oblige me, and it is important that she should be correctly dressed for what she has to do."

Josie looked curiously at what Eva was wearing at the moment as her mistress went on:

"She requires something smart and very ladylike to wear tomorrow for luncheon. You understand, Josie. She is a *jeune fille*, and must not in any way be flamboyant."

"I know exactly what *M'mselle* needs," Josie replied. "When I was with the Ambassadress I was in England for three years and *Oh là* the English *jeunes filles* are dowdy, drab and dull!"

She was speaking in French, thinking perhaps that only her mistress would understand.

Then Eva burst out laughing.

"*Mademoiselle* speaks perfect French, Josie," Leonide Leblanc said.

"*Pardon, M'mselle,*" Josie said. "I did not mean to be insulting!"

"What you said is true," Eva said. "I understand because my mother was French, and often said the same thing!"

Then as she thought she had been indiscreet she looked at Leonide Leblanc.

"A slip of the tongue," Leonide said, "but remember in future to be very careful. Your mother was English, and your father was French."

"I . . I will remember," Eva said.

"Now, hurry, Josie, and put on your bonnet," Leonide Leblanc said, "for I shall want you back because you must help me dress."

"*Mais oui, Madame* I shall be very quick."

She went from the room and Eva rose to her feet.

"What can I say?" she asked.

"You will thank me by doing exactly what I have told you," Leonide Leblanc replied. "Lord Charles is a dear friend of mine and I wish to please him. I also want to help you because of your father. And as it is, everything is very satisfactory!"

"Very . . very . . satisfactory!" Eva agreed.

She took Leonide Leblanc's hand, then impulsively bent forward to kiss her.

For a moment the Frenchwoman seemed surprised. Then she smiled.

"You are very sweet," she said, "and I hope, one day, you will marry somebody as nice as your father, and be very, very happy."

"That is what I have always wanted," Eva replied.

CHAPTER THREE

Josie was on the whole quite complimentary about Eva's clothes.

They were very simple, but as she said, correct for a *jeune fille*.

However, as a Frenchwoman, she could not resist adding little touches of *chic*.

Eva thought they made all the difference.

A bow on the shoulder, lace round the sleeves and a few silk flowers on the hem of the skirt.

They transformed what had been a very ordinary gown into something which might easily have been worn by a young French girl.

"Thank you, thank you," Eva said.

Looking at the clock Josie said she must return to *Madame* Leblanc.

She had obviously been impressed by the elegance of the house.

Now she looked round her and said in the voice of a disapproving Nanny:

"You should not be living here alone, *M'mselle*!"

"But I am very happy, even though I miss my father," Eva protested.

"*Vous êtes très belle*, and you need a chaperon."

"I have already promised *Madame* that I will behave

48

in a very circumspect way," Eva said defensively. "I will pretend that my Aunt, who is very strict, is in bed with a cold."

Josie laughed.

"*M'mselle* is clever, but you are very young."

"I will get older," Eva said, "and if things are too difficult, I will go back to England."

She was not quite certain what she meant by "too difficult".

It must somehow involve men who would want to kiss her.

The men whom Leonide Leblanc had warned her against.

"Once I have done what Lord Charles requires of me," she told herself consolingly, "then I shall not be meeting any Social people. I shall visit the *musées* and try to paint a picture which will be saleable."

On thinking it over she thought that was the only way she could make money.

It would now prevent her from becoming involved with men.

Her mother had praised her water colours.

When she had tried her hand at oils, she had, after many mistakes, produced quite a good portrait.

It was of one of her father's horses.

She wondered if she could afford to have lessons, knowing there must be many artists in Paris who could teach her.

Then she knew that to be concerned with Artists, Poets and Writers who were to be found on the Left Bank might be dangerous.

More so, she felt than being involved with the Social World which her father had enjoyed.

"I shall just have to be like Papa and hope that 'something turns up'," she told herself philosophically.

She was, however, so excited by the idea of earning so much money that she found it hard to sleep.

Only when dawn was breaking did she fall into a heavy slumber.

She dreamt that she was riding a fast horse.

She was being pursued round a race-track by a lot of strange men who were also on horse-back.

She woke up and laughed at her dream.

As she dressed she knew she felt elated, as if something very exciting was about to happen.

At the same time, she felt very nervous in case she did anything wrong.

She sent up a little prayer to her father saying:

"Please . . Papa . . help me! You will know what Lord Charles is like, and also *Monsieur* Bischoffheim. You must prevent me from saying . . anything which will . . spoil *Madame* Leblanc's plans."

She arranged her hair very carefully and put on the gown that Josie had pressed.

Although she was not aware of it, it made her look very young and innocent.

It was white with a full skirt, and a bodice which just showed the curves of her figure.

Josie had added a little bow of blue ribbon on the shoulder.

There was another on the opposite side of her waist.

A little round hat sat on the back of her head like a halo, with blue ribbons trailing down her back.

She was getting ready to walk, as she had yesterday, to Madame Leblanc's house in the *Rue d'Offemont*.

Henri came upstairs to knock on the door.

"*Entrez*," Eva called out.

Henri came in.

"There's a carriage arrived for you, *M'mselle*," he said.

"For me?" Eva exclaimed in surprise.

Then she realised who had sent it, and added:

"How very kind of *Madame* to think of me!"

She drove off feeling very grand in the most elaborate and spectacular carriage she had ever seen.

It was only then that she remembered she should not have walked alone through the streets yesterday to visit *Madame* Leblanc.

Her mother had told her that when she went to London to shop, or if she walked in the Park, she would have to be accompanied by a house-maid.

"How tiresome, Mama!" Eva had exclaimed at the time.

"I agree with you," her mother said, "but it would not be at all *comme il fait* for a *jeune fille* to wander about alone."

When they had first come to Paris her father had accompanied her everywhere.

It had therefore never crossed her mind that she should not walk about the streets without somebody being with her.

This created a problem for the future.

Marie was getting on in years.

Eva was quite certain that having already been to market, she would not wish to venture out again.

The horses trotted quickly through the streets.

Eva found herself thinking despairingly that, once she was alone, there would be a great many difficulties

The carriage drew up outside *Madame* Leblanc's house.

The footman on the box opened the door with a flourish.

The Butler whom she had seen yesterday smiled at her.

"*Bonjour, M'mselle!*" he said. "*Madame*'s expecting you if you'll go upstairs to her bedroom."

51

Eva walked up the stairs, knocked on the door and heard Leonide Leblanc call out: "*Entrez!*"

She went in, expecting to find her in bed, as she had been yesterday.

But she was dressed and, while Josie was arranging her hair, she was putting the finishing touches to her face.

She had looked fascinating yesterday.

But now Eva saw she was very smart and very elegantly dressed.

It would be impossible, she thought, for anyone who saw her not to stare at her in astonishment.

Her gown was certainly too flamboyant to be worn by any Englishwoman.

Not only was her face powdered and painted, but she had added mascara to her eye-lashes, and her lips were crimson.

What was more, she was wearing a necklace, ear-rings, and bracelets of rubies and diamonds.

They glittered in the sunshine.

They made her whole appearance not only striking, but also theatrical.

"*Bonjour*, Eva!" Leonide Leblanc said.

She turned from the dressing-table at which she was sitting.

She was looking at Eva's appearance, and now she said:

"*Tres bien*! You look exactly as I would want you to do, and I can see that Josie had added French *chic* to your shoulder and your hair."

"She was very kind and helpful," Eva said.

As they were talking, Josie brought from another room a hat which Leonide Leblanc was going to wear.

It was the same colour as her gown.

52

It was covered with ospreys which shimmered with every move.

It was so fantastic that Eva stared at it and Leonide Leblanc said with a smile:

"I am going for my drive in the *Bois*. The carriage which brought you here will be open. Every day I appear in a new *toilette* and generally with a new livery for my servants!"

"You look marvellous!" Eva exclaimed.

Leonide Leblanc laughed.

"Now perhaps you understand why, when you leave here with Lord Charles, you must never admit to knowing me."

"But, why?" Eva asked.

"Be sensible, my dear," Leonide Leblanc replied. "Can you imagine your mother or your mythical Aunt who is in bed with a cold being seen dressed like this?"

Because the way she spoke was so funny, Eva laughed.

"No, *Madame*, and if they did so in London they would stop the traffic!"

"That is what I try to do in Paris," Leonide Leblanc said complacently. "In fact, there are quite a number of people who go to the *Bois* specially to see me!"

Josie put the hat on her head.

"I do not think this outfit is as smart as the one I wore the day before yesterday," Leonide Leblanc complained.

"I like it better, *Madame*!" Josie said firmly. "And you said yourself that the black coachmen in a white livery were a mistake."

To Eva it sounded fantastic, but she said nothing.

She was aware that Leonide Leblanc shrugged her shoulders.

Josie pinned the hat to her hair with long hat-pins which were encrusted with diamonds.

She rose, still looking at her reflection in the mirror.

"I am bored with these rubies," she said. "Send them back to my jeweller and tell him to re-set them."

"Very well, *Madame*," Josie said in a resigned tone as if this was something she did frequently.

"Tell him to send the bill to the *Duc* or, better still, I will get him to give me a necklace of emeralds. I am tired of the one I possess already."

Leonide Leblanc did not wait for an answer.

She merely walked towards Eva saying:

"Lord Charles is downstairs and we have kept him waiting long enough. Now remember, you are a girl who has fallen on hard times. You need money, but you are a Lady, and outside this house you know nothing of women like myself."

She spoke with a mocking note in her voice, but Eva said:

"I know that you are very kind, *Madame*, and that I shall always remember you in my prayers."

For a moment Leonide Leblanc was still.

Then she said quickly:

"Come along, come along! I have to drive in the *Bois* and you and Lord Charles must have a little talk before you go to visit *Monsieur* Bischoffheim."

They went down the stairs, and a man-servant opened the door into the Salon.

Leonide Leblanc swept in.

Lord Charles, who had been sitting on the sofa reading a newspaper, rose to his feet.

"I thought you had forgotten me," he said.

"How could I do that?" Leonide Leblanc replied.

As she spoke, Eva thought there was a different note in her voice from the way she had been speaking to her.

She could not describe it, but it was somehow, for want of a better word, 'Caressing', and Eva thought, "inviting".

54

Leonide Leblanc gave Lord Charles her hand and he raised it to his lips.

For a moment Eva thought they were speaking to each other without words.

Then Leonide Leblanc said quickly:

"Now I want you to meet Eva Venarde, who has promised to help you and will, I know, do exactly what you require of her."

Eva had walked in somewhat slowly behind Leonide Leblanc.

Lord Charles had not even glanced at her.

Now he stared at her.

She thought it was in a somewhat insulting manner before he exclaimed:

"Leonide, you are brilliant! I called you a genius, but now I know you are a Genie, and can magic up everything a man could desire!"

Leonide Leblanc smiled at him before she said:

"You are not to frighten Eva. She has never done anything like this before, and you have a great many things to explain to her."

"You are leaving?" Lord Charles asked.

"Why do you think I am dressed like this?" Leonide enquired. "My public is waiting, and I must not disappoint them!"

"I will see you to your carriage."

He put his hand under her arm and drew her across the room.

Only when she was alone did Eva think that he had in fact, been rather rude to her.

Undoubtedly he was very good-looking in a typically English manner.

At the same time, he frightened her.

As she waited for his return she wished she did not have to do anything so complicated to earn £500.

Then she told herself she was being very ungrateful.

What other girl would have had such a splendid opportunity?

"I can stay in Paris," she said beneath her breath, "and live in my perfect little house so I must be sensible and not complain whatever happens."

Lord Charles came back into the room and she was still standing where he had left her.

He smiled at her pleasantly, then said:

"Let me compliment you or shall I congratulate Leonide ? You look exactly as I wanted you to look!"

"Thank you!" Eva said. "And I hope I will not make any mistakes."

"Suppose we sit down and talk about it?" Lord Charles suggested. "I have ordered a bottle of champagne, and I think a drink is what we both need."

Eva looked at him in surprise.

She supposed that gentlemen like Lord Charles started drinking early in the day.

She was certain it was something of which her mother would not approve.

The servant must have had the champagne ready.

He came into the room with a bottle and poured out two glasses.

He handed one to Eva from the gold salver, then another to Lord Charles.

Eva took it because she thought it would be a mistake to refuse.

She only took a tiny sip.

Then she set the glass down on a small table near the sofa.

When they were alone again Lord Charles said:

"I suppose Leonide has told you why you are doing this to help me?"

"I am pretending . . to be your . . *fiancée*," Eva said

a little hesitatingly, "but I think you should . . tell me how long we have known each other . . and if we met in France . . or in England."

"In France!" Lord Charles said firmly. "If Bischoffheim talks about you to any of my English friends, they will think it strange they have not heard of you before."

"Oh, I understand," Eva exclaimed, "and *Madame* Leblanc said I was to say that my father was French."

"That I think would account for the fact that according to Leonide, you speak French perfectly, which Bischoffheim would not expect of an English girl."

"You make it much clearer for me to understand," Eva said.

"What I want to do," Lord Charles went on, "once we have established the fact that we are engaged to be married and Bischoffheim has coughed up what he owes me, is to make certain there will be no more difficulties."

"I . . I hope not," Eva said.

"You sound doubtful," Lord Charles exclaimed. "What is worrying you?"

"Nothing really," Eva replied, "except that my mother always said I was a very bad liar, and I am afraid of . . letting you down."

Lord Charles laughed.

"I am sure you will not do that, and Leonide, who is an excellent judge of character, assured me that you would be perfect in the part."

He drank some more of the champagne. Then he said:

"You look stunning! How on earth did Leonide find anyone like you at such short notice?"

Eva was just about to say that she had called on her, then thought perhaps it would be a mistake.

Instead she said:

"I think it would be wrong for me to remember anything except that I am your *fiancée* and we are looking forward to being married."

Lord Charles looked at her sharply. Then he laughed.

"So you are being evasive! You are quite right! Of course, keep your secret and, as you say, we must stick to the script."

He glanced at the clock on the mantelpiece.

"Bischoffheim asked us to be there early," he said, "so I suggest we drive to his house which, as you can imagine, is very luxurious and important, and is in the *Champs Elysées*."

"Is he so very, very wealthy?" Eva asked.

"He is as rich as Midas, and everything he touches turns to gold," Lord Charles replied. "It is said the whole Empire would collapse without him, and certainly the members of the *Bourse* grovel at his feet."

"You sound as though you do not like him," Eva said.

Lord Charles smiled.

"I have a great affection for his money," he replied

He said it in a way which made Eva laugh.

Then as Lord Charles rose to his feet he remarked:

"You have not drunk your champagne!"

Eva was about to say that she did not want it so early in the morning, but instead she replied:

"I do not think your *fiancée* My Lord . . would drink, except on special occasions."

"You are quite right," Lord Charles agreed. "At the same time, you need not keep up this pretence when we are alone."

He paused a moment and then went on:

"I find you very interesting and lovely, and I want to hear the true story of why, looking like you do, you are not as rich as Leonide."

58

Eva did not understand what he was implying, so she merely said:

"I expect the real answer is that I am not as clever as she is."

As she spoke she walked out of the Salon and therefore did not see the look in Lord Charles's eyes.

The carriage waiting outside for them could in no way be compared to Leonide's.

The roof was open and the coachman driving it was properly dressed.

But Eva thought it was just the kind of vehicle which might have been hired from a superior Livery Stable.

The two horses which drew it were certainly not to be compared to those owned by Leonide Leblanc.

Eva, however, thought it was a mistake to ask questions.

As they drove along she realised that while Lord Charles seemed at his ease, he was in fact slightly nervous.

Because she was curious, she could not help asking:

"If *Monsieur* Bischoffheim is really angry because you will not marry his daughter, what will happen about the horses you have bought for him?"

"He could refuse to pay for them," Lord Charles replied, "in which case, I shall have to look for another buyer, or find myself bankrupt, unless my brother rescues me."

He spoke violently, and Eva knew it was a very real fear.

Because she felt sorry for him, she said:

"I am praying, I am praying very hard that does not happen. I am sure, because it is wrong for *Monsieur* Bischoffheim to thrust his daughter on you, that my prayers will be heard."

"I certainly hope you are right," Lord Charles said,

"and it is very kind of you to take so much interest in my affairs."

"I am also thinking of myself," Eva said honestly.

Lord Charles looked at her curiously.

"Can £500 really mean so much to you?" he asked, "when you look as you do? There must be dozens of men wanting to give you that amount of money, and a great deal more besides!"

Eva's eyes opened until they seemed to fill her whole face.

Then she said:

"I do not know many men . . and I certainly could not . . accept money from one . . unless I earned it."

She sounded so shocked at the idea that Lord Charles thought, if she was acting, she was certainly a brilliant performer.

"Where the devil did Leonide find her?" he asked himself, "and how can she look the part, besides talking as she does?"

He, however, had no more time for introspection for they had arrived at Raphael Bischoffheim's house.

It stood among the trees in a large garden.

It had formerly belonged to a French aristocrat of the *ancien régime*.

He had been unable to afford to keep it up and had therefore retired to his *Château* in the country.

Bischoffheim had bought for a bargain one of the most outstanding houses in Paris.

They entered through the iron gates which were heavily tipped with gold.

Eva thought that everything she looked at seemed to portray wealth.

The red carpet that ran down the stone steps was thicker and softer than any carpet she had trodden on before.

There were six footmen in the hall.

They wore a fantastic livery, decorated with gold braid.

The Major Domo was even more brilliantly attired.

He escorted them across the hall, and having asked Lord Charles their names, opened a door.

"*M'mselle* Eva Venarde and Lord Charles Craig, *Monsieur*!" he announced in stentorian tones.

Because she was frightened, for a moment Eva felt the room swing in front of her eyes.

Then she realised that what was dazzling her were the enormous crystal chandeliers, the gold-framed chairs and sofas, and the mirrors.

These were set in gold carved frames.

The pictures which would have graced any Museum were also framed in gold.

Raphael Bischoffheim, who had been standing by the mantelpiece walked towards them.

When she could focus her eyes on him, Eva saw that he was short, with shining dark hair and heavy eye-brows.

He must have been over fifty, but he was slim and moved quickly.

He put out his hand to Lord Charles saying:

"It is delightful to see you, My Lord, and of course, I am ready to welcome your friend?"

There was, although Eva did not realise it, a question-mark after the word 'friend'.

There was also a suspicious expression in *Monsieur* Bischoffheim's eyes, as if he thought that Lord Charles had brought with him a young woman who would not be welcome in his mother's Drawing-Room.

Lord Charles, understanding the implication of his words merely replied:

"And it is delightful to be here, *Monsieur*. May I introduce to you *Mademoiselle* Eva Venarde?"

There was a confidential note in his voice as he added:

"We will let you into a little secret, which you must promise not to reveal to anybody for the moment. It is that *Mademoiselle* and I are engaged to be married!"

Raphael Bischoffheim was too good a businessman to show any surprise.

Yet Lord Charles, who was watching him closely, was aware that it was something he had not expected.

It took him a second or two to adjust himself to an entirely new and unexpected situation.

Then he said, and his quiet voice did not sound anything but sincere:

"I am extremely gratified that you have taken me into your confidence, and of course I will not speak of your engagement until you allow me to do so."

"You have to understand," Lord Charles explained, "that I have not yet broken the news to my brother, or to the rest of my family."

He smiled at Eva before he added:

"As soon as they know, we shall be arranging our marriage, and of course, sending you an invitation."

"Which I shall be delighted to receive!" *Monsieur* Bischoffheim replied. "Let me be the first to congratulate you and of course I must drink to your health!"

They moved towards the fireplace.

At the moment, and Lord Charles knew it had been planned in that way, *Mademoiselle* Jael Bischoffheim came into the room.

She was, as it happened, quite a good-looking girl, even though she resembled her father.

Her rather big nose was off-set by two very large dark eyes in a small oval face.

"Ah, here you are my dear" Raphael Bischoffheim said in an over-hearty tone. "I want you to meet Lord Charles Craig and a friend of his, *Mademoiselle* Eva Venarde."

They all shook hands.

A somewhat stilted conversation followed until luncheon was announced.

Because they were only a party of four Lord Charles realised that Raphael Bischoffheim had been contriving very cleverly how he would meet his daughter.

Then when luncheon was over and before they left for the stables, he would put forward the proposition that he should marry her.

As it was, Lord Charles talked to his host about the horses he had purchased for him.

He told him from which stables they had come, emphasising not only their breeding, but also that of their owners.

Eva realised she must talk to Jael Bischoffheim.

But she found the girl was shy.

She was also obviously terrified of saying anything which would incur the wrath of her father.

Before any answer she made to a question she glanced at him to see if he was listening, or to evoke his approval.

By the end of luncheon Eva was convinced that *Monsieur* Bischoffheim was a bully.

Just as he extorted money from those outside his home, so he demanded obedience inside it.

The food was excellent, and the wine the best and most expensive a French *Vignoble* could supply.

When luncheon was finished, Lord Charles told Raphael Bischoffheim that the horses would be waiting for them in his stables.

"Then we must go to see them," *Monsieur* Bischoffheim said. "I suppose, if they wish, the young women can stay here."

Before Lord Charles could speak, Eva said:

"Oh, please, let me come with you. I love horses,

and I have heard so much about those that have come to France for you."

"Then of course you must accompany us," *Monsieur* Bischoffheim agreed. "And what about you, Jael?"

"I have a Music Lesson, Papa," his daughter replied.

She spoke convincingly, but Eva felt she had already been told that she was not wanted.

They left Lord Charles's vehicle behind and set off in a swift, well-sprung carriage belonging to their host.

Everything about it was shining and it was almost as spectacular in its way as Leonide Leblanc's.

Eva longed to ask if the accoutrements; the lamps, the bridles, the door handles and everything else, had been made of real gold.

She thought, however, this might sound impertinent and annoy *Monsieur* Bischoffheim.

They reached the stables which were just on the out-skirts of Paris.

Once again they were luxury personified.

Eva had the feeling that even the horse-rugs were made of thicker and better wool than those in other stables.

Certainly the stalls were as luxurious as a room in the Tuileries Palace!

Monsieur Bischoffheim already had a number of horses.

None of them compared however with those that Lord Charles had brought from England.

He might be annoyed that his plans for his daughter's marriage had come to nothing.

But he could not disguise his delight at becoming the owner of such outstanding animals.

They were in the stall of the stallion which Lord Charles had bought from the Royal Stud when the Head Groom said:

"You've got visitors, *Monsieur*!"

Monsieur Bischoffheim turned round and at the same time Lord Charles glanced over his shoulder.

Then he exclaimed in English:

"Hello, Warren! I did not expect to see you here!"

"I heard you were in Paris, Charles," the newcomer replied.

An extremely handsome man, he was over 6' tall with broad shoulders and athletic hips.

Eva thought he would have been recognised as an Englishman wherever he went.

There was something vaguely familiar about his face.

Then Lord Charles said:

"I do not think, *Monsieur* Bischoffheim, that you have met my brother the Duke of Kincraig!"

"No, indeed," *Monsieur* Bischoffheim replied, "and I am delighted to make Your Grace's aquaintance."

"And I am anxious to see your horses," the Duke replied. "The *Comte* tells me you have one of the most outstanding stables in France."

"That is what I hope to have," *Monsieur* Bischoffheim replied.

The Duke looked back to where the Gentleman who had accompanied him was giving orders to one of his servants

Now he came forward to say:

"Forgive me, Bischoffheim, how are you? It is nice to see you again."

"And delightful to see you, *Monsieur*!" the Banker replied.

The Duke looked to his brother:

"I do not think, Charles, that you have met the *Comte* de Chabrillin with whom I am staying!"

"No, but I have heard of him!" Lord Charles replied holding out his hand.

As the Duke spoke, Eva started and stared at the newcomer.

He was a man of about fifty, very distinguished and at the same time obviously French.

"So this," she thought to herself, "is Mama's brother, and my Uncle!"

Then she was aware that the Duke was staring at her, and Lord Charles said slowly:

"Let me introduce my brother, *Mademoiselle* Eva Venarde!"

Eva curtsied and *Monsieur* Bischoffheim said:

"This is a momentous occasion, and something I did not expect to take place in my own stables!"

The Duke looked surprised.

"Momentous?" he questioned.

Monsieur Bischoffheim put his fingers to his lips.

"*Tiens!*" he exclaimed, "now I have made a *faux pas*! How tiresome of me! You must forgive me, Lord Charles, but I had completely forgotten that you told me your engagement was a secret!"

As he spoke, Eva was quite certain that he had not forgotten what he had been told.

He was however deliberately and because he was annoyed, making trouble for Lord Charles.

She was sure now that he would buy the horses.

At the same time, his plans for his daughter's marriage had gone awry and he had no intention of letting Lord Charles get away with it.

"Engaged?" the Duke repeated. "Why have I not been told about this, Charles?"

It was quite obvious that he was annoyed, and Lord Charles replied quickly:

"I have not yet had time, and in any case, I had no idea you were in France."

"Well, now that the 'cat is out of the bag'," the

Comte de Chabrillin interposed, "of course we must celebrate."

He paused to smile at his brother, before he went on:

"As I am sure you would wish your *fiancée* to become better acquainted with your brother, let me invite you to dine with me tonight."

There was nothing Lord Charles could do but say that they would be delighted.

Then, as if he thought he had stirred up enough trouble, *Monsieur* Bischoffheim began to praise volubly the horses which had come from England.

Eva followed the gentlemen round with no one paying any attention to her.

She had therefore the chance of looking more closely at her Uncle.

She could only feel it was a strange quirk of Fate, but one which undoubtedly would have made her father laugh.

While she was pretending to be somebody else she had met the Head of her mother's family!

CHAPTER FOUR

Driving back from *Monsieur* Bischoffheim's house to her own, Eva was alone with Lord Charles.

"How could *Monsieur* Bischoffheim behave so badly," she asked, "in telling your brother of our engagement when he had promised he would not?"

"He was getting his own back!" Lord Charles replied. "He is known to be a hard, vindictive man, and he certainly has made things difficult for me!"

Eva gave a little sigh.

"Perhaps I should not . . dine with the *Comte* tonight," she said.

As she spoke, she knew it was something she wanted very much to do.

It was fascinating to see one of the mother's relatives.

She had always been curious about the whole family.

Lord Charles thought for a moment, then he said:

"I think that would be a mistake."

"Why?" Eva asked.

"Well, first of all, my brother would think you were avoiding him, and secondly, as Bischoffheim will be there, he might be suspicious about our engagement."

"I did not realise that the *Comte* had also invited *Monsieur* Bischoffheim," Eva remarked.

"I heard him do so when he was saying goodbye," Lord Charles replied. "After all, he could hardly be the only one of the party to be left out."

"No . . of course not," Eva replied.

"The *Comte* has a house near the *Bois*," Lord Charles said, "so I will call for you at about a quarter to eight. We are not dining until half-past."

He spoke in a somewhat disagreeable voice.

Eva knew he was upset that his brother should have been told of his 'engagement'.

There was silence until Lord Charles said:

"Damn Bischoffheim! This is sure to be embarrassing, and as he has not yet given me the cheque, there is nothing either of us can do but make ourselves pleasant."

"But surely he cannot refuse to pay you now?" Eva asked in a frightened tone.

"Bischoffheim is so rich that he is a law unto himself," Lord Charles replied, "and as you have already seen, we cannot trust him; so for God's sake, do not make any mistakes!"

"I will try . . not to," Eva replied.

At the same time, she was nervous.

One of the gowns which Josie had altered for her had belonged to her mother.

While it was in a more sophisticated style than her own, it was in a very pale shade of Parma violet.

Of soft chiffon in a simple style, it had a *chic* about it which her own gowns did not have.

As she put it on, Eva thought that it might have belonged to Leonide Leblanc.

But she would doubtless have had magnificent amethysts to wear with it round her neck, and also in her ears.

Then she laughed and thought that jewellery was not important.

She had her own perfect little house and would have enough money to keep it going for a long time.

She had to arrange her own hair.

Then she found some velvet ribbon amongst her mother's belongings which were the same colour as the gown.

She tied it in a bow round the curls that she had arranged at the back of her head.

She thought that she had achieved the same style that Josie had created on *Madame* Leblanc.

There was a wide scarf of the same velvet to wear over the gown.

When Lord Charles arrived she stepped into his carriage.

"You look lovely," he exclaimed as they moved off, "as I expect all the men at dinner tonight will tell you, with the exception of my brother!"

"Do you . . think he . . disapproves of me?" Eva asked.

"I am sure he does," Lord Charles replied. "I saw the expression on his face when Bischoffheim said we were engaged, and I am quite certain he is going to be difficult."

He spoke in such a worried tone that Eva said:

"I . . I am sorry."

Then Lord Charles laughed.

"It will be all right," he said, "and as soon as Bischoffheim pays me, I can tell Warren the truth and force him to admit that I did the only thing possible in the circumstances."

Eva had the feeling as he spoke that the Duke would be very difficult to force into doing anything.

There was something commanding about him.

She did not say anything, and Lord Charles remarked as if to himself:

70

"There is nothing else we can do."

They were driving in the same carriage which Lord Charles had used during the day.

But Eva had noticed that the coachman was different and was certain she was right in thinking it came from a Livery Stable.

They drove up the *Champs Elysées* and had almost reached the *Bois* when the horses turned into a small drive.

It was in front of what to Eva appeared to be a large attractive house.

Her mother had told her a lot about the *Comte*'s *Château* in the country where she had lived as a girl.

But Eva could not remember her mentioning a house in Paris.

She was, however, for the moment more interested in the *Comte* than in his possessions.

He was waiting for them in a large Salon.

It over-looked the gardens at the back of the house.

It was beautifully decorated, Eva thought, and very French.

The *Comte* looking smart in his evening clothes, which were a little different from those worn by the Duke and Lord Charles, held out his hand.

"I am delighted you are here, *Mademoiselle*," he said. "I have always admired your fiancé's knowledge of horses, and no one is better informed than your future brother-in-law."

While he was paying these compliments, Eva was aware that the Duke was scowling.

There was certainly no admiration in his eyes as he looked at her.

"I am very fortunate this evening," the *Comte* went on, "in having another expert on horses whom I think you all know, as my guest."

As he spoke a man came into the room.

He looked distinguished, middle-aged, and had an air of authority about him.

Eva was not surprised when he was introduced as the *Marquis* de Soisson.

He was obviously on very friendly terms with the Duke.

"Congratulations, Jacques!" the latter said. "I see that two of your horses won last week, and I suspect you are already thinking of winning the Gold Cup at Ascot."

The *Marquis* laughed.

"Dare I aim so high?"

"Why not?" the Duke asked, "and, quite frankly, I think you have a very sporting chance!"

"In which case I shall certainly try," the *Marquis* replied.

He had shaken hands with Lord Charles and *Monsieur* Bischoffheim before the *Comte* said:

"And now, *Mademoiselle* Venarde, I must introduce you to one of our most important 'Patrons of the Turf' – the *Marquis* de Soisson!"

Eva curtsied and the *Marquis* put out his hand, and she lay her fingers in it.

As she did so she found he was looking at her as if he was surprised by her appearance.

When they went into dinner, she was seated on the *Comte*'s right.

The *Marquis* was on her other side.

To her annoyance, because she wanted to listen to what her Uncle was saying, the Ma*rquis* did his best to monopolise her.

He paid her compliments, and there was a look in his eyes which she felt was definitely impertinent.

The *Comte* was exchanging a joke with the Duke.

While he did so the *Marquis* said in a voice that only she could hear:

"With whom have you come, and when may I see you again?"

Eva looked at him in astonishment and was silent.

"I suppose you came with Bischoffheim!" the *Marquis* went on. "He has a *penchant* for very beautiful young women!"

It was then Eva realised that there was no other woman at the dinner-table.

This had therefore given the *Marquis* entirely the wrong idea about her.

Perhaps he thought she was an actress.

Or else like Leonide Leblanc, she could defy the conventions because she was not really a Lady in the full sense of the word.

She could not tell him she was engaged to Lord Charles in case he should spread the falsehood further.

At the same time, she knew that she should answer his question.

"I . . I came here with Lord Charles Craig," she said coldly.

"*Nom de Nom!*" the *Marquis* swore. "This is not the first time that Charles has 'pipped me at the post'!"

A burst of laughter from the other side of the table concealed his next words which were:

"I suppose you know he has no money?"

Eva did not know what to do.

Then quickly, she turned towards the *Comte* saying:

"I am sure that was a very amusing joke, but the *Marquis* was speaking to me, so I did not hear it!"

The *Comte* smiled.

"You have missed nothing that would be suitable for your young ears," he said, "and now, *Mademoiselle*, you

73

must tell me about yourself. Does your family live in Paris?"

Eva shook her head.

"No, I am only staying here for a short time, and I live in the South near Vence."

She had thought while she was dressing what she should say if this particular question was asked.

She remembered reading a book about Vence and how beautiful it was.

"Then you do not often come North?" the *Comte* said.

"This is really the first time," Eva replied.

"Then you have never visited any of the *Châteaux* South of Paris?"

"It is something I would love to do," Eva replied.

"Lord Charles will tell you that mine in particular is very attractive," the *Comte* smiled.

"Oh, do tell me about it!" Eva pleaded.

She was anxious to hold him in conversation. She knew that if he turned away from her she would have to listen to the *Marquis*.

"My *Château* was built at the same time as Vaux-le-Vicomte," the *Comte* said, "of which doubtless you have read about in the History Books."

"Yes, I have," Eva said eagerly.

In fact, it was her mother who had told her about Vaux-le-Vicomte.

It was when she had been describing the *Château* belonging to the Chabrillins.

"Then of course you know that it was Le Vau who designed the *Châteaux* which set the fashion for the Courtiers of Louis XIV to own fantastic *Châteaux* within reach of Paris."

Eva was listening intently, and he said unexpectedly:

"I can see you are interested, so instead of listening

74

to me, why do you not come to see my *Château* for yourself?"

Eva gave a little gasp.

"I would love to do that more than anything else in the world!" she exclaimed.

"Then it is something you must certainly do," the *Comte* replied.

He looked down the table at Lord Charles and said:

"As your brother is staying with me, Lord Charles, and this charming lady is very anxious to see my *Château,* I suggest you bring her down tomorrow and stay for at least two nights before returning to the gaieties of Paris."

Watching Lord Charles, Eva saw him hesitate.

Then as if he thought it would be a mistake to refuse, he replied:

"That is very kind of you, *Monsieur* and I am sure it is something we will both enjoy."

Because she had been willing him to accept, Eva gave a sigh of relief.

Then as she turned her head she realised that the *Marquis* was looking at her in astonishment.

"What is all this about?" he asked, "and what will *Madame la Comtesse* have to say?"

"I hope, *Monsieur*, she will be pleased to see me," Eva said primly.

The *Comte* was continuing his conversation with her.

There was no chance for the *Marquis* to say any more.

In French fashion, they all left the Dining-Room at the same time.

Soon after they had moved into the Salon, *Monsieur* Bischoffheim said he had promised to look in on a party that was being given by one of his friends.

As he said goodnight to Lord Charles he said:

"I am afraid I shall not be in Paris tomorrow, but if you will call on me as soon as you return from your visit to the *Comte* we can conclude our business transaction."

Listening, Eva knew that Lord Charles was annoyed.

Once again Bischoffheim was delaying paying him the money he owed.

There was nothing he could do, however.

She thought as *Monsieur* Bischoffheim walked jauntily away that he was enjoying keeping Lord Charles on tenterhooks.

They did not stay very much longer, and as Lord Charles drove Eva home, he said:

"Why on earth did you get the *Comte* to invite us to stay with him? If we had remained in Paris, I could have received the money the day after tomorrow."

"I . . I am . . sorry," Eva replied, "he was talking about his *Château* and I really . . did want to hear . . about it."

Lord Charles did not say anything, and to excuse herself she went on:

"The *Marquis* de Soisson was interested in the reason why I was at the party when there were no other ladies present."

Lord Charles looked at her in surprise.

"Why? What did he say?" he asked sharply.

"He asked me if I was with *Monsieur* Bischoffheim and said he wanted to . . see me again."

"I can understand what he was thinking," Lord Charles said, "but if you will take my advice, you will have nothing to do with him. He has a nasty reputation."

"That is . . what . . I thought," Eva murmured.

"Of course, he is rich," Lord Charles went on, "and, as you well know, that covers a multitude of sins, but there must be lots of other men waiting for you who are far better than him!"

Eva did not understand what he was saying.

Because she did not wish to talk about the *Marquis* any further, she changed the subject.

"It may be very annoying for you,"she said, "but I am very anxious to see the *Château* of the *Comte* de Chabrillin, and we need stay only one night."

"Yes, of course," Lord Charles replied, "and I have no intention of staying any longer, as we will have to cope with my brother."

"Perhaps it would be . . wiser to tell him . . the truth," Eva suggested in a small voice.

She was thinking that if Lord Charles did so, he might then think it unnecessary for them to stay with the *Comte*.

In which case, she would not be able to see the *Château* where her mother had lived.

Lord Charles considered this for a moment, then he said:

"No, I think that would be a mistake. Warren is the type of man who will never tell a lie if he can possibly avoid it, and if by some mischance Bischoffheim should learn that we have been deceiving him, the 'fat would be in the fire'!"

"Then we must be very, very careful!" Eva said.

"We will be," Lord Charles agreed, "and we will leave my brother in ignorance, but for God's sake, be careful what you say."

"Then . . please . . do not leave me . . alone with him," Eva begged.

"I will do my best," Lord Charles said, "but you know what these French households are like – too many people with too much to say!"

Eva laughed.

She could not reply that she had never been in a French household.

She therefore had no idea what it was like.

. . . .

The following day, Eva woke up with a feeling of excitement.

By the sheer hand of Fate, she was going to visit her mother's home.

It was something she had never expected to be able to do.

When she thought about it, she was sure that the Family Chabrillin would have been annoyed that her mother had been left a house in Paris by her grandmother.

They had never made the slightest sign that they wished to meet her father or, for that matter, her.

"It is really very strange that I should enter their house under a false name," Eva thought.

She felt a little shiver go through her in case she was exposed.

That would not only make her Uncle the *Comte* angry but also Lord Charles and his awe-inspiring brother the Duke.

"Please . . Mama . . help me," she prayed.

She knew that her mother was the one person who could do so.

She thought she ought to tell Leonide Leblanc that she was going away, but there was no chance of her doing so.

Before Lord Charles said goodnight he arranged to collect her at eleven o'clock the next morning.

Eva knew she had to pack her clothes.

She also had to make sure that she had all the right things to wear in the country.

It was no use expecting any assistance from the old servants.

78

She managed by getting up early to press the country clothes that had been packed up since she arrived in Paris.

Then she repacked them.

By the time she had finished she only just had time to tidy her hair and put on a pretty gown.

It was one which was not too smart for the country and she found a hat to match it.

Remembering what Leonide Leblanc had said to her, she was waiting in the hall when Lord Charles arrived.

When he appeared she said a little breathlessly:

"I am sorry I cannot ask you in, but my Aunt, who is staying with me is not very well, and has had breakfast in bed."

"Your Aunt!" Lord Charles exclaimed.

She thought his eye-brows were raised.

But he did not say any more.

Nor did he seem to think it strange that she had spoken to him in English.

This was because she did not wish Henri to overhear what she said.

He had been standing in the hall, and he now carried her trunk outside.

Eva saw that instead of the carriage they had used yesterday, Lord Charles had a very smart Curricle.

She wondered if he had hired it or bought it.

It certainly had two well-bred horses to pull it.

When they set off with the groom sitting up behind, Eva was aware that he drove very well.

He did not seem to have much to say to her.

They therefore were silent until they were out of the traffic and Eva was thinking how lovely the countryside was.

Driving beside the Seine, they passed fields already green with the Spring crops.

"It is lovely!" Eva exclaimed involuntarily.

"That is what I always think when I come to France," Lord Charles replied. "You should however, be used to it as you live here."

"But every part of France is different," Eva said evasively.

"Yes, of course," he replied, "and I understand why Artists come here in their droves!"

He made what he said sound so funny that Eva laughed and said:

"When they see the *Comte's Chateau* they must either paint a picture of it or write a poem."

"Personally, I am more interested in a piece of paper called a cheque!" Lord Charles remarked. "We shall have had quite enough of the *Comte* and his *Château* by midnight tonight, and I intend to leave early tomorrow morning, so do not over-sleep."

"I will be ready at whatever time you wish," Eva replied.

She spoke so gently that Lord Charles looked at her as if for the first time.

"You are a very accommodating young woman!" he said. "It is only that things are not working out exactly as I intended. I nearly had a stroke yesterday when my brother walked into Bischoffheim's stables!"

"You sound as if you are frightened of him!" Eva remarked.

"Of course I am!" Lord Charles replied. "You would not understand, but in England the Head of a family like yours holds the title, the estate and all the purse strings!"

"Do you really mean '*all*'?" Eva asked.

"I depend on my brother for every penny I possess," Lord Charles replied savagely. "And at the moment, I possess nothing but a mountain of debts!"

"It sounds very . . frightening!"

"It is!"

He drove on a little way before he said:

"Warren is obviously annoyed at my getting engaged without telling him, to somebody who has nothing to recommend her except her looks!"

It made her sound of so little worth that Eva said tentatively:

"Perhaps it would be better if we pretended that I was an heiress until we can tell him the truth."

Lord Charles laughed, but there was no humour in it.

"That would be too dangerous," he said. "The French, who love money, are well aware who has it and who does not. My brother would know that, if Bischoffheim had been aware you were hung with golden shekels he would have mentioned it."

Eva was silent, and after a moment Lord Charles said:

"We just have to sit it out until tomorrow, and once I have cashed that all-important cheque, we can breathe again."

"Then I can only repeat," Eva said in a small voice, "please do not . . leave me alone with the Duke. If he cross-examines me . . he will guess that I have not told him the . . truth."

"That is something he must not do!" Lord Charles said sharply, "and, incidentally, what you are paid to prevent, so watch your words, and do not get us into any more of a mess than we are in already!"

There was nothing Eva could say, and they drove on in silence. But she felt depressed.

It was only when the *Château* finally came in sight that she felt better.

It was exactly as she had expected it to be with its towers, fountains and formal gardens.

As they drove up to the front door she felt as if her mother was with her telling her that in a way she had come home.

They arrived just before luncheon-time and the *Comte* greeted them effusively.

A servant brought them aperitifs.

While the men were talking, Eva went to the window to look out at the garden.

It was just as her mother had said a French garden would look like, but words were inadequate beside the beauty of the reality.

There was a huge fountain playing in the centre.

There had been smaller fountains at the approach to the house.

The one in the garden was exquisitely carved and the water gushed from a huge cornucopia held by a cupid.

As it rose iridescent into the sunshine, Eva held her breath.

"I hope my garden, and also my *Château* come up to your expectations, *Mademoiselle!*" she heard the *Comte* say beside her.

"It is lovely . . perfectly lovely!" she exclaimed. "Just how I knew it would be!"

He raised his eye-brows.

"You have heard of my *Château* before, or were you just anticipating your visit?"

"Both," Eva answered, "and it is lovely to think that anything so beautiful survived the Revolution and must be today just as it was when it was first built."

After she had spoken she thought perhaps she had been indiscreet.

It was her mother who had told her that, strangely enough, the *Château* was not devastated during the Revolution

"I think the truth was," she had said, "that the people

in the village were so fond of the *Comte* who lived at the time that they not only spared his life, but also his house."

"There is a great deal more for you to see," the *Comte* was saying, "and now, here is my wife. I know she is looking forward to meeting you."

Eva was then introduced to a charming woman whom, she learned later, came from a distinguished family, the equal of the Chabrillins.

The *Comtesse* sat at the top of the large table in the Dining-Room, and the *Comte* was at the other end.

They both looked very aristocratic and distinguished.

Eva could understand why the family had been disappointed when her mother, who was so beautiful, had run away.

Especially as it was with a man who, at the time was an unimportant Englishman.

As her mother had told her to expect, there was a number of relatives staying in the house.

There were also the six children of the *Comte* and *Comtesse*.

Three of them were grown up, and the ages of the others ranged from twelve to eighteen.

They were all, Eva thought with satisfaction, extremely good-looking.

They all had dark hair.

Although she thought somebody might have noticed the resemblance to her mother in her face and eyes, her hair and complexion was certainly different from that of her cousins.

At luncheon they all chatted away to everybody in the delightfully informal manner characteristic of the French.

Eva found it charming.

At the same time, she was aware that the Duke was staring at her in a somewhat hostile manner.

When they arrived he had greeted both her and his brother coldly.

After the meal was finished, the *Comte* said:

"Now I want to show you my horses, and I am hoping, Lord Charles that *Mademoiselle* Venarde will not find them too inferior to those magnificent animals you have brought from England."

"I scoured the country for the best!" Lord Charles replied.

"That was obvious," the *Comte* said, "and I only wish I could afford anything as good, but unfortunately, I do not have Bischoffheim's reserves!"

The two men laughed as if that was a joke.

The they walked through the garden towards the stables.

Eva wanted to linger and inspect the fountain, but she also wished to see the horses.

She was accompanied by one of her older Cousins, who was telling her unasked the history of the family.

She was sure it was something strangers always wanted to know.

"And what do you do?" Eva asked when he paused for breath.

"I intend to be a Politician," he said, "but do not tell Papa! He thinks that Politics are a bore, while I find them intriguing."

Eva laughed.

"I will keep your secret, and I agree with you that politics are always exciting."

"If you are interested in History," her Cousin said, "I must tell you about the cannon which you see at the end of the garden."

They walked on.

84

Eva longed to tell him that she knew the history of the cannon as well as he did.

The *Comte's* horses were good, very good.

Yet they certainly did not equal those which they had seen in Raphael Bischoffheim's stables.

"If you have made certain he will win every race, Lord Charles," the *Comte* said, "there will be no point in us poor owners competing for the *Grand Prix* or any other race!"

"I think you are being very pessimistic," Lord Charles replied. "After all, while Bischoffheim may be able to buy the best, he does not know a great deal about horses. It is the right training and choosing the right Jockey that win races."

The *Comte* put his hand on Lord Charles's shoulder.

"That is very wise of you, young man," he said, "and I am sure your brother appreciates how much you know about the 'Sport of Kings'."

"Charles is undoubtedly an expert in his own field," the Duke said rather grudgingly.

'He is unpleasant in more ways than one!' Eva thought indignantly.

She was being very careful to keep as far away as possible from him.

There was a great deal to see during the afternoon.

Then, accompanied by Pierre, who was the same Cousin who had escorted her before, she went into the Library.

Unexpectedly the Duke joined them.

"Your mother is looking for you, Pierre," he said.

"I said I would try to find you. She is in the *Salon Bleu.*"

There was nothing Pierre could do but go to his mother.

With a sinking of her heart, Eva realised that although

she had tried to avoid it, she was now alone with the Duke.

"You are interested in books, Miss Venarde?" he asked.

"Very!" Eva replied. "But I have never before been in such a magnificent Library."

"I would rather, at the moment, talk about you," the Duke said.

"I . . I wonder where . . Charles is?" Eva asked quickly.

She remembered only just in time that Lord Charles had said as they neared the *Château*:

"Do not forget to call me by my Christian name! You would hardly address the man to whom you are supposed to be engaged as 'My Lord'."

"Charles is at the moment with our host," the Duke said, "and you cannot continue, Miss Venarde to keep running away from me!"

Eva blushed.

She was not aware that he had noticed her efforts to avoid him.

There were two sofas one on either side of the huge mediaeval fireplace, and the Duke said:

"Suppose we sit down?"

There was nothing Eva could do but obey him.

As she did so she glanced at the door praying that somebody would appear to join them.

"First of all," the Duke began, "tell me about your family. I feel my brother has been very remiss in not even informing me of your existence."

"He intended to do so when he returned to England," Eva replied.

"But I am here," the Duke said, "and it would make things far easier if you would tell me about yourself."

"I . . I do not think there is . . very much to tell," Eva said. "Both my parents . . are dead."

That, at any rate, she thought, was true.

"I am sorry! It must be very sad for you to be alone."

"I miss them . . both very much!" Eva replied.

"I believe, although I may be mistaken, that you are not wholly French?"

"No, my mother was English."

"English!" the Duke repeated. "And what was her name?"

Eva had already thought of this, and because she did not wish to tell more lies than was necessary, she replied:

"Hill. Her maiden name was Hill."

"There are a great many Hills in England," the Duke remarked. "It is, in fact quite a common name. Where did your grandparents live?"

"In . . in Gloucestershire."

"You have been to England?"

"Yes"

"And did you like it as much as France?"

"I love both countries," Eva answered, "and after all, there is only the Channel to divide them."

The Duke smiled.

"That is a good way of putting it, but it is of course a division, and I am just wondering, Miss Venarde, or perhaps, as you are to be my sister-in-law, I should call you Eva, if you will enjoy living in England."

"I look forward to it!" Eva said defensively.

"I expect Charles has already warned you that it will be in somewhat straitened circumstances, unless of course, you have money of your own?"

Eva felt she was getting out of her depth.

She was frightened of what she might have to say next, and rose to her feet.

"I hope Your Grace will forgive me," she said quickly, "but I really must go to find our hostess. She promised to show me some of the . . State Rooms, and she will think it rude if I keep her waiting . . too long."

She did not wait for the Duke to answer.

Dropping him a curtsy she moved swiftly towards the door.

Even if he had called after her she would not have heard him.

When she reached the passage she ran towards the hall and up the stairs to the First Floor.

Only when she reached the bedroom into which she had been shown on her arrival did she feel for the moment that she was safe.

"He frightens me!" she told herself, "and it is a good thing that I am not in love with Lord Charles, as I am certain he intends by some means or other to break up our 'engagement'."

She sat down on the stool in front of the dressing-table and looked at her reflection.

"Perhaps if he knew who I really am, he might not be so antagonistic," she went on, "he thinks I am not good enough for his precious brother – and Papa would consider that an insult!"

CHAPTER FIVE

When dinner, which had been a very talkative and amusing meal was over, the *Comte* said:

"I expect you gentlemen will want to play cards."

There was a murmur of assent from his sons and from Lord Charles.

Speaking to him the *Comte* said:

"As you tell me that you and *Mademoiselle* Venarde are leaving early tomorrow morning, I am going to take your *fiancée* to the picture Gallery. She cannot leave without seeing the portraits of my ancestors."

His children laughed at that and teased him, and Eva said:

"You know I want to look at everything in the *Château* which is the most fascinating building I have ever seen."

"You see there is one person who admires my obsessions!" the *Comte* said to Pierre, who replied:

"We are all as proud as you are, Papa, but we do not say so much about it!"

"Go and play cards, you cheeky boy!" the *Comte* replied.

He drew Eva out of the Salon, and they walked to where, at the end of the *Château* was a long Gallery.

Like everything else, it was beautifully arranged.

The pictures started with the *Comte*'s first ancestors.

Gradually they went round the Gallery until it ended up with a recent *"Tableau de Genre"*.

It was of himself, his wife and his children.

Many of the names were familiar to Eva.

The *Comtes* de Chabrillin had been celebrated Statesmen, Courtiers, and Generals.

They had therefore been her heroes since she was a small child.

She was listening attentively to everything her Uncle told her.

They moved slowly from portrait to portrait.

Finally with a leap of her heart she realised she was looking at the face of her mother.

Lizette had been painted when she was seventeen.

Before the *Comte* spoke Eva guessed it was when she had become officially engaged.

She stood looking at the portrait seeing her own eyes, her own nose and her own lips.

The main difference was that her mother's hair was dark.

Also her skin had not the same pink-and-white transparency which was very English.

Because it meant so much to Eva she forgot for the moment that the *Comte* was with her.

She could only look at her mother, feeling almost as if she spoke to her.

Then, as if the *Comte* became aware of her special interest in the portrait, he said:

"This is my sister Lisette, who I am afraid, caused something of a scandal in the family when she ran away with an Englishman."

Eva did not speak, and he went on:

"As you can see, she was very lovely, and I only regret that I did not see her again before she died."

90

Eva drew in her breath.

She tried to prevent the tears from coming into her eyes.

She had always found it difficult to speak of her mother without wanting to cry.

Now her portrait seemed to be speaking to her.

She needed all her self-control to prevent herself from breaking down.

Then, as if the *Comte* was aware of her attention, he looked at her.

Suddenly there was an incredulous expression on his face.

His head turned from her to the portrait and back again.

Finally, as if he was speaking to himself, he cried:

"The likeness is incredible! I knew there was something familiar about your face, but I could not think what it was!"

Eva gave a little gasp, but before she could speak the *Comte* said:

"Is it possible – can you be Lisette's daughter?"

Eva looked towards the door as if she was afraid somebody was listening.

Then she said pleadingly:

"Please . . do not say . . any more! It is a secret . . and nobody here has any . . idea of it."

The *Comte* stared at her.

"Are you telling me that you *are* my niece, and you are engaged to Lord Charles, but he has no idea you are my sister's child?"

Eva nodded.

"Please . . please, do not . . ask any more . . questions."

The *Comte* smiled.

"Do you really expect me to be inhuman? Now that

I have found you, that I must not talk to anyone about it?"

"But . . you must not . . you must not!" Eva said. "If I tell you the reason . . will you swear to me on . . your honour that you . . will not tell . . Lord Charles or . . the Duke?"

"I will promise anything you ask," the *Comte* said, "at the same time, I insist on knowing the whole story."

He reached out and took her hand in his.

Then he looked up at the portrait and said quietly:

"I think it is something your mother would want you to do."

Because he spoke gently and kindly, Eva felt the tears run down her cheeks.

Quickly she wiped them away.

The *Comte* drew her back to the end of the Gallery where there was a comfortable sofa and several chairs.

He sat down on the sofa and drew her down beside him.

"First I must tell you," he said, "how deeply I regret that I never saw your mother after she had run away with your father."

"Mama was . . very sad that she had . . lost her family," Eva replied, "although she was . . ecstatically happy with . . Papa."

"Unfortunately, I was not here when it happened," the *Comte* continued. "I was five years older than she was, and in the Army. Shortly after she ran away I was sent to Africa with my Regiment."

"Mama told me all about . . you and her . . other brothers and sisters. That was why I was so . . thrilled to . . come to see the . . *Chateau*."

"I can understand that," the *Comte* replied. "I thought

from the first you were very lovely, and now I know why you appealed to me was because you resemble my beautiful sister."

Once again Eva wiped away a tear, and he said:

"You must not cry, but tell me what has happened to your father and why you are here with Lord Charles?"

It was difficult for her to speak without crying.

Eva wiped her eyes because the tears embarrassed her.

Then she told him how her father had died of a heart-attack.

She related how she had gone to collect his shirt-stud from Leonide Leblanc.

She went on to explain how *Madame* Leblanc had arranged for her to save Lord Charles from having to marry *Monsieur* Bischoffheim's daughter by pretending to be his *fiancée*.

She was not aware that the *Comte* stiffened when she spoke of Leonide Leblanc.

Then when she spoke of *Monsieur* Bischoffheim's intentions he exclaimed:

"I have never heard anything so disgraceful! How dare Bischoffheim attempt to blackmail Lord Charles into marrying his daughter!"

"You will understand," Eva said, "why Lord Charles was trying frantically to avoid the situation. At the same time, he is still desperately afraid that *Monsieur* Bischoffheim will not pay him what he is owed."

"You had no other contact with Leonide Leblanc, except that she was a friend of your father's?" the *Comte* asked.

"She was very kind to arrange that I should be paid so much money," Eva answered, "which means that I can continue to live in that beautiful house which my grandmother left to Mama."

The *Comte* smiled.

"Certain members of the family were very disappointed when they found it was not left to them."

"I was . . afraid they would feel . . like that," Eva said, "but I love it . . too, and I want to be . . able to go on . . living there."

"We will talk about that another time," the *Comte* said. "But *now* I want you to know that you are always welcome here, and I think my wife will prove a better chaperon than the Aunt you are pretending to have with you."

Eva looked at him wide-eyed.

"Do you . . do you . . really . . mean that?"

"Of course I mean it," the *Comte* replied.

"But . . please . . you must not say anything to anyone . . until Lord Charles receives his cheque."

"I can understand now," the *Comte* said, "that is the reason why he wishes to return to Paris tomorrow morning."

Eva nodded.

"Very well, my dear," he said, "you must go back with him and as soon as everything is settled, we will meet and talk about your future."

"You are kind . . very kind," Eva murmured. "I know that is what Mama would want . . for me. At the same time . . I do not wish to be an . . encumbrance on you any more . . than . . I would impose myself on my father's relatives."

"As you can see," the *Comte* smiled, "there is plenty of room here and you can certainly use your house in Paris whenever you wish, as long as you take one of my family with you."

He gave a laugh before he said:

"I can assure you they will be only too willing to be your guests. My older children all have a yearning for Paris, and have often complained that there is not enough room for them in my own house."

He patted Eva's hand as he said:

"Do not worry your head about that for the moment, just fulfil your obligation which I can quite understand you must do, to Lord Charles. Then we will have luncheon together the day after you are free."

"Until then you . . promise you will . . say . . nothing to . . anybody?"

"I assure you as a Chabrillin I never break my word," the *Comte* said, "and as your blood is the same as mine, I realise that you cannot break yours."

"I know that is . . something Mama would . . expect you to say," Eva said, "and thank you . . thank you for being . . so kind!"

"I have not had an opportunity of being kind yet," the *Comte* replied, "but I feel I owe you a great deal that I should have expended on your mother."

He gave a deep sigh.

"But regrets are a waste of time, and my only excuse for neglecting Lisette in the past was that my father was a hard man. He never forgave her and for years he would not have her name mentioned."

"But you remembered her," Eva said, "and I am sure it will make her happy to . . know that we have . . met each other . . now."

"I know it will," the *Comte* said, "and never again, my beautiful niece, are you to think you are alone and obliged to seek the help of somebody like Leonide Leblanc."

There was a note in his voice which told Eva how much he disapproved of *Madame* Leblanc.

She thought perhaps it was because she was so theatrical and as her mother would have said, did not look like a Lady.

"But she was very kind to me," she thought, "and I must express my gratitude, although I am not quite certain how."

The *Comte* glanced at the clock over the mantelpiece.

"I suppose we must go back to the others, and it is time for you to go to bed," he said. "There is so much more I want to hear about your mother, and I shall look forward eagerly to our next meeting."

"So shall I!" Eva said.

They both stood up, then the *Comte* bent and kissed her on the cheeks.

"You are very lovely, my dear," he said, "and every time I look at you I shall feel it is like having your mother with us again."

They walked down the Gallery and only when they reached the door did Eva say:

"You will be very, very careful in front of Lord Charles, and the Duke? I am sure they would be shocked at what I have done if they knew I was Papa's daughter."

"Of course they would," the *Comte* agreed, "and it is something which will never happen again. Thankfully it will be over once Lord Charles has been paid."

Eva smiled at him.

They walked in silence into the Salon where the male members of the party were still playing cards.

Some of the women, however, had already retired.

Eva slipped away.

When she was in bed she prayed for a long time, telling her mother how wonderful it was to be in the home she had loved so much.

Now she need no longer worry about the future.

"I know it is . . all due to you . . mama, and of course Papa, who always . . believed that 'something would turn up'. I am lucky . . so very, very lucky!"

When she fell asleep she dreamed she was talking to her mother.

They were sitting together in the Salon downstairs under the crystal chandeliers.

. . . . . .

Eva had told her maid to call her early.

She also thought it would be quicker if she had breakfast in her room.

She had only just finished and was putting on her hat when she was told that Lord Charles was waiting for her.

She could understand his haste to be back in Paris.

As two footmen hurriedly carried her trunk away from her room she ran down the stairs.

There was quite a number of the Chabrillin family to say goodbye to her.

The *Comtesse* kissed her and said:

"I hope when you are married, my dear, you and your husband will come to stay with us. We have so enjoyed having you!"

"Thank you, *madame*. Every moment has been a delight!" Eva replied.

The *Comte* helped her into the Curricle, saying as he did so:

"I feel it will not be long before we meet again, *Mademoiselle* Venarde!"

His eyes were twinkling as he spoke and his fingers pressed hers.

Eva knew that she was amused at the pretence they were keeping up in front of Lord Charles.

"Thank you! Thank you for everything!" she cried

She knew he understood.

As they drove off she looked back to see at least six of her relatives still standing on the steps waving to them.

"They are charming," she thought, "and I love them so much already."

Lord Charles was driving swiftly and exceedingly well.

Eva knew he was determined to reach Paris and bring his business transaction with *Monsieur* Bischoffheim to an end.

Because she was curious she could not help asking:

"You will not say . . anything to him about our 'engagement?'"

"Certainly not!" Lord Charles said. "You are not likely to have any contact with him but if you do, just be dignified and refuse to answer any questions."

Eva thought that might be difficult, but she did not say so.

They drove on.

When they reached her small house he hastily put her trunks down in the hall.

Lord Charles drove away.

He had said as she got out of the curricle:

"I will see you later in the day."

At the same time, he did not say "thank you" which she thought was somewhat unkind.

She only hoped there would be no more difficulties or obstacles in the way of him being paid.

Then she could revert to being herself.

As her Uncle had suggested she could stay at the *Chateau.*

She was so happy at the idea that she wanted to sing and dance.

She ran up the stairs to change from the clothes in which she had driven back as if she had wings on her feet.

She came downstairs again, wearing a gown that Josie had made smart enough for Paris.

It was then she thought that now she should visit Leonide Leblanc, and tell her that everything had gone well.

Leonide had known her father.

She was the only person who would understand how much it meant for her to be accepted into the Chabrillin family.

"I must tell her at once!" Eva thought.

Then she remembered she was not supposed to walk in the streets without having somebody with her.

But when she enquired where Marie was, she learnt that she had gone to market.

She knew that Henri, who was suffering from rheumatism, could only walk very slowly.

Anyway he would have no wish to leave the house.

"What will it matter?" Eva asked, "if just this once I walk alone?"

She hurried off.

Because she was intent on where she was going, she had no idea that anyone had noticed her.

Nor that men turned round to take another look at her.

When she reached Leonide Leblanc's house, it was luncheon-time.

She was aware that she felt rather hungry.

'Perhaps Leonide Leonide will offer me something to eat,' she thought.

When he opened the door the man-servant smiled at her.

"*Bonjour M'mselle*! If you wish to see *Madame* she is in bed and alone."

"I am very anxious to see her," Eva replied, and ran up the stairs.

Leonide Leblanc was in bed, looking more fascinating than ever.

She wore a transparent pink nightgown and pink ribbons in her hair.

"My dear, I am delighted to see you!" she exclaimed. "I have been wondering what has happened and whether you would let me know if everything went according to plan."

"Not quite," Eva replied, "but very well."

She sat down on the chair beside the bed, and told Leonide Leblanc exactly what had happened.

She listened without speaking until Eva had finished, then she said:

"*C'est extraordinaire! Comme un conte de fées!*"

"That is what I thought myself," Eva replied.

"How fortunate that the *Comte* is your Uncle, now the *Comtesse* will chaperon you and find you an acceptable husband."

"I have no wish to marry, at least not for the moment," Eva replied, "and only when I can find somebody as charming and amusing as Papa."

Madame Leblanc sighed.

"*Hélas*, but men like that are few and far between! But now you are safe, and nobody will insult you when they know you are under the protection of the family Chabrillin."

"I cannot think why anyone should want to!" Eva objected, "except perhaps the Duke, who is very curious, and I think a little hostile."

"Forget him!" Leonide Leblanc said. "He will go back to England, you will be in France and never meet him or Lord Charles again."

"Charles is very grateful to you for saving him," Eva said, "I am sure he would never have thought of anything so clever on his own."

"What you are really saying is that he would never have found anyone like you!" Lenoide said, "but now

you must forget this little escapade, and do not talk about
it to anyone except your Uncle."

"No . . of course not," Eva agreed.

There was a knock on the door and the man-servant
asked:

"Do you require your luncheon, *Madame?*"

"Yes, and at once!" Leonide replied, "and *Mademoiselle* Venarde will have it with me."

She looked at Eva and added:

"I have the idea that nobody has asked you to
luncheon?"

"Nobody!" Eva laughed.

"Then we shall eat together and after that, we must
say goodbye, for you realise you must never tell anybody
that you have met me."

"I told my Uncle."

"I expect he was shocked, even if he did not show it."

Eva thought this was very likely true.

She still did not understand why, but aloud she said:

"I shall always remember how kind you have been,
and although you say I must not see you, I think Papa
would want me to love you and always be very, very
grateful that it was through you I found my Uncle."

"I told you it is a Fairy Story!" Leonide said, "and
now all you have to do is to live happily ever after!"

They laughed and talked all through the very delicious luncheon which was brought upstairs on elegantly
arranged trays.

Then when the meal was finished Eva said goodbye.

"I wish there was something I could give you," she
said. "Can you think of anything you would like?"

She looked around the flower-filled room and remembered the beautiful objects d'art she had seen in the
Salon.

"You seem to have everything!" she added.

"What I would like," Leonide said, "is for you to send me just sometimes a little momento of what you are doing – the announcement of your Marriage, the printed Marriage Service when it takes place, and of course, photographs when you have them, of you and your family."

"Of course I will send you those things," Eva cried, "and every time I post them to you, I shall remember it here, and all that happened because of you."

Leonide Leblanc held out her arms.

"*Adieu*, my most charming and lovely little friend. Do not forget – you must never say that you have been here in my house. But just remember me sometimes in your prayers."

"You know I will do that," Eva said.

She kissed her affectionately.

She turned back to wave as she reached the door.

As she did so she thought there was something wistful in Leonide's expression.

She took one last look at the orchids which seemed to fill the hall.

She had a glimpse of many more through the open door of the Salon.

Then the man-servant let her out and she walked down the steps and out into the street.

She hurried home, knowing it would be a mistake to linger at the shops.

When Henri opened the door she said:

"I am back, Henri! Has anybody called?"

"No, *M'mselle.*"

Eva ran upstairs to take off her hat.

She was hoping that nothing had gone wrong with Lord Charles's interview with *Monsieur* Bischoffheim.

If it had, she thought she would still have to go on pretending to be his *fiancée*.

That could mean she would not be able to have luncheon with her uncle tomorrow.

"I pray everything has gone well," she thought. "But surely Lord Charles could have let me know by now? Unless once again, *Monsieur* Bischoffheim is keeping him waiting!"

She went downstairs to the salon which seemed very small after the enormous one in the *Château*.

But they were very like each other.

She knew from what her Uncle had said that it was her grandmother who had made the *Château* so attractive.

Her taste must have been impeccable.

Eva stood in front of a glass cabinet admiring some pretty little Dresden china figures.

She heard the door open.

She turned round eagerly thinking it would be Lord Charles.

To her astonishment, the *Marquis* de Soisson came into the room.

She stared at him incredulously before she asked:

"Why . . are you . . here? What do you . . want?"

He smiled before he said:

"I will answer your first question, which is that, quite by chance I was driving down the *Rue d'Offement* when I saw you come out of a certain house which is, of course, the most famous in the whole street!"

Eva stared at him thinking how much she disliked him.

She also knew by the tone of his voice that he thought he had been very clever in discovering something about her.

"I followed you back here," the *Marquis* continued, "and now, *Mademoiselle* Eva Venarde, we can put out cards on the table, and you can stop deceiving me, however cleverly you have deceived Lord Charles!"

"I do not know . . what you mean," Eva answered, "and as . . my Aunt who is . . chaperoning me is . . upstairs in bed, I must ask you, *Monsieur* to leave . . immediately."

The *Marquis* laughed.

"So that is your little game! Well, my dear, you do not 'pull the wool' over my eyes, and as a friend of Leonide, I assure you you can no longer keep up the pose of being a Social débutante."

"I asked you to leave, *Monsieur*!"

"Which I have no intention of doing, until you listen to what I have to say."

"I cannot imagine that you will say anything I want to hear," Eva said, "and I can only ask you to behave in a proper and civilised manner and leave me alone!"

The *Marquis* sat down on the sofa.

"Now stop playing games," he said, "and let me tell you exactly how I feel. I want you and I intend to have you!"

"I have no . . idea what you . . mean," Eva replied.

She was in fact, speaking truthfully, but at the same time, she was frightened.

There was something in the way the *Marquis* spoke.

Also the expression in his eyes told her he was dangerous.

She was not certain, however, what she could do about it.

She knew that by now Henri would have returned to the kitchen.

Even if she asked his help in turning the *Marquis* out of the house, he was an old man.

He would be incapable of standing up to somebody like the *Marquis*.

She wondered frantically what she should do and as she hesitated the Marquis said:

104

"Come and sit down like a sensible girl, and hear what I have to say to you."

Because she appeared to have no alternative, Eva did as he asked.

She moved towards a chair as far away from the *Marquis* as possible.

However he made a gesture with his hand towards the sofa where he was sitting.

She thought it would seem childish not to obey him.

She sat as far as she could from him.

He leaned back, very much at his ease with one arm along the back of the sofa.

"You are incredibly lovely!" he said, "in fact when I first saw you, I thought you could not be real, but a figment of my imagination!"

Eva did not answer and he said:

"I cannot think you have been in Paris long, or I would have met you before Craig did. However, if he is the first man in your life, I intend to be the second!"

"I . . I am engaged to be . . married . . to Lord Charles," Eva said.

The *Marquis* laughed, and it was a very unpleasant sound.

"That is what I learnt from Bischoffheim, and quite frankly, I do not believe a word of it!"

Eva looked at him in horror.

He must have upset *Monsieur* Bischoffheim by telling him that she and Lord Charles were not really engaged.

Perhaps that was why Lord Charles had not brought her the cheque as he had promised to do, and the whole deal might be off.

Because the idea was so terrifying, she said:

"Surely, you did not . . say anything so . . untrue . . to *Monsieur* Bischoffheim?"

"As it happens, I do not!" the *Marquis* replied.

Eva heaved a sigh of relief.

"But I watched you and Craig together, and I thought there was something 'fishy' about the whole thing, besides the fact that you got yourself invited to Chabrillin's *Château*."

"I cannot think why you should . . suspect that there is anything . . wrong about our engagement!" Eva managed to say.

"I knew I was right, my pretty one," the *Marquis* said, "and absolutely right when just now I saw you coming out of Leonide's house. Now tell me exactly what your game is! And if you ask me, you are backing the wrong horse!"

Eva made a little gesture with her hand.

"What you are . . saying is quite . . incomprehensible!"

"Nonsense! You understand every word!" the *Marquis* said. "You thought Craig was rich, and you pursued him, and because he is a rather stupid young man he promised you marriage!"

He paused a moment and seemed to leer at her as he went on:

"You will not marry him – you can be quite certain of that – not when his brother finds out about you. So you had better 'cut your losses'!"

What he was saying, and the way he was speaking, made Eva feel bewildered.

Then before once again she could ask him to leave, the *Marquis* said.

"Now what I am offering you is a far better proposition I am a very rich man, and when I get what I want, very generous. I suppose this house is rented, but I will give you one of your own, a carriage with two horses and all the jewels you can put round your pretty neck! What do you say to that?"

He spoke in a flamboyant manner as if he thought she would find what he was saying irresistible.

"I think .. *Monsieur* .. you are .. insulting .. me!"

The Marquis laughed.

"You know as well as I do that you will find it difficult to be offered more, unless you were Leonide, which you are not! Now, come along, let us have no more playing about!"

He reached out his hand towards her as he spoke.

Because Eva realised he was going to touch her, she jumped to her feet.

"Go away!" she said, "go away .. from me! You are .. horrible! Bestial! I refuse to .. listen to any .. more!"

Because she was frightened, she spoke frantically.

Then as the *Marquis* rose she realised how large and powerful he was.

She took a step away from him saying:

"Leave .. me .. alone!"

"That is something I have no intention of doing," he replied. "And let me tell you, I like little birds who flutter and defy me. I find it very exciting to capture them!"

He reached out towards her.

Once again Eva backed away from him only to find there was a chair directly behind her.

It was impossible to go any further.

The *Marquis* put his arms around her and pulled her roughly against him.

She gave a cry, and started to struggle with him.

Attempting to thrust him away with her hands.

She was also moving her head from side to side as she tried to prevent him from kissing her.

"You excite me!" he said in a low, deep voice, which

sounded like the growl of a wild animal. "I want you, and by God, I mean to have you!"

It was then Eva screamed.

As she did so she felt his lips, hot and demanding, against the softness of her skin and she screamed again.

CHAPTER SIX

The Duke had not said good-bye to Eva and Lord Charles for the simple reason that he had already left the *Château*.

He had an important appointment in Paris.

He therefore rode across country on one of the *Comte*'s fastest horses.

He sent his luggage and his Valet by road.

When he arrived at the house near the *Bois* he had a bath and changed his clothes.

Having eaten a large English breakfast he left to keep an appointment with the Emperor.

He had messages for Louis Napoleon from the Prince of Wales, and also the Prime Minister.

Then, because they were old friends, the Duke and the Emperor sat talking for over half-an-hour.

The Duke returned to the *Comte*'s house and was sitting at a desk writing a letter when his brother burst into the room.

"I have got it! I have got it!" Lord Charles shouted. "Now there need be no further problems!"

The Duke smiled.

"I gather you were somewhat apprehensive in case Bischoffheim did not pay up."

His brother put the cheque down on the blotter in front of him.

The Duke saw that it was made out for £15,000.

"No wonder you were worried!" he remarked. "How much of this is yours?"

"Nearly £9,000," Charles replied.

"Will that pay all your debts?"

"The most pressing of them. There will however, be a number left over."

The Duke was silent, and Charles looked at him questioningly. Then he said:

"I will pay the rest."

Charles stared at him.

"Do you mean that, Warren?"

"There is, naturally, a condition attached."

"What is that?" his brother asked anxiously.

"That you will leave for London immediately."

"Why?"

"I should have thought that was very obvious," the Duke replied. "Your friend Leonide Leblanc will certainly need some of this, and quite frankly, you cannot afford the women of Paris."

"As it happens," Charles said defensively, "Leonide has never charged me so much as one *franc*."

"Then you have been lucky. But if she sees this amount of money, she will undoubtedly want a present."

"I suppose you are right," Charles said reflectively. "At the same time, I owe her something for producing Eva."

The Duke stiffened.

"What do you mean by that?"

"I was going to tell you once Bischoffheim settled up!" Charles said. "I was given a tip-off that he intended to blackmail me into marrying his daughter!"

"The Devil he was!" the Duke exclaimed. "How could you possibly do such a thing!"

"It is something I have no intention of doing," Charles retorted, "but if I had refused, he would have threatened not to pay the money I had already expended on the horses."

"It is the most disgraceful thing I have ever heard!" the Duke said, "the man is a complete outsider."

"I know that," Charles agreed, "but I had to defeat him at his own game, and it was Leonide who produced Eva like a rabbit out of a hat!"

The Duke did not speak and Charles gave a little laugh before he went on:

"You will hardly believe it, but she made me swear on my honour that I would 'leave the girl exactly as I found her.'"

"What did she mean by that?" the Duke enquired.

"In her own words – 'pure, innocent, and untouched'," Charles answered.

The Duke raised his eye-brows, and his brother said:

"I have kept my word, and I promised Leonide that I would give Eva £500."

He expected his brother to make some comment, but the Duke merely took a cheque from his wallet.

"I will cash Bischoffheim's cheque immediately, at the Bank I use in Paris," he said. "You will take mine for the same amount to London."

"And Eva?" Charles asked.

"I will see to her, and I will also send Leonide Leblanc something she will appreciate in your name."

"Warren, you are a sportsman!" Charles exclaimed, "and do you really mean you will pay my debts?"

"I have said I will pay them," the Duke replied, "but try to be a little more sensible in future. As you can imagine, I have been wondering how you could keep a wife on credit!"

Lord Charles laughed.

"You well know it would be impossible, unless we were happy to live in a tent."

"Well, that at any rate, will be unnecessary," the Duke said in a tone of relief.

"I cannot begin to thank you . . " Charles began.

The Duke looked at his watch.

"If you do not catch the one o'clock train to Calais, I might change my mind."

Charles gave an exclamation of horror.

At the same time, he was laughing.

"I will catch it," he promised, "and drink your health all the way to Dover!"

"Before you go," the Duke said, "you had better give me the address of Eva Venarde."

Charles explained where the house was in the *Rue St Honoré* and the Duke said:

"Let me advise you – on no account tell the story of what has occurred to anybody! It would be a great mistake."

"But I am longing to say that I have 'pulled a fast one' on Raphael Bischoffheim!" Charles protested.

"As I imagine he could be a very vindictive man, and money always speaks louder than laughter, it is something you would regret."

"You are right – of course you are right," Charles agreed, "but I really have got the better of him."

"Then keep it to yourself," the Duke advised.

As Charles went from the room the Duke could hear him shouting for the curricle in which he had travelled to the country.

"He is incorrigible!" he said to himself, but at the same time he was smiling.

He realised even better than Charles did that Bischoffheim was not a man to be trifled with.

112

He therefore drove immediately to a Bank in the *Rue de la Paix* which was affiliated to his Bank in London.

He paid in the cheque for £9,000 and collected £500 in *francs*.

Then he drove to his Club.

After a light luncheon, the carriage which belonged to the *Comte* carried him to the house in the *Rue St. Honore*.

An elderly servant opened the door.

The Duke stepped into the hall he heard Eva scream.

Without waiting for Henri who, as usual, was moving very slowly, he walked swiftly to the door of the Salon and walked in.

One glance told him that Eva was fighting desperately against the *Marquis* de Soisson.

Neither of them realised that anyone else had come into the room.

Then when Eva gave another helpless, pitiful little scream of an animal caught in a trap the Duke acted.

He sprang forward, catching hold of the *Marquis* by the back of his collar, and pulled him away from Eva.

"What the hell do you think you are doing?" he asked.

For a second both the *Marquis* and Eva looked at him in sheer astonishment.

Then Eva threw herself against the Duke.

"Save me . . save . . me!" she cried and his her face against his shoulder.

The *Marquis* released himself from the Duke's grasp and pulled the lapels of his coat back into place.

"Why are you here? And what has it got to do with you, Kincraig?" he enquired.

"Get out!" the Duke said sharply.

113

The *Marquis* went crimson in the face.

"I have as much right here as you have," he replied

"I told you to leave," the Duke said.

"And if I refuse?" the *Marquis* asked aggressively.

"Then I am quite prepared to use forceful means to evict you," the Duke said coldly.

Because he did not raise his voice his threat was far more effective than if he had shouted.

He was much taller than the *Marquis*.

There was also an expression in his eyes which had made many men quake in front of him.

With a muttered oath the *Marquis* turned on his heel.

He walked out of the Salon slamming the door behind him.

The Duke did not watch him go.

He merely looked down at Eva who was still hiding her face on his shoulder.

He was aware that her whole body was trembling.

Gently he moved her to the sofa and helped her to sit down on it.

She was very pale, and he was aware that the expression in her eyes was one of shock.

"It is all right," the Duke said. "The *Marquis* has gone, and I doubt if he will come back."

"But . . if . . he does?" Eva faltered, and shivered.

The Duke glanced round the room.

"Are you living here alone?" he enquired.

Because she was so shattered by what had happened, Eva told him the truth.

"Y.yes."

The Duke looked surprised. Then he asked:

"And whose house is it?"

"It is . . mine."

Now the Duke was definitely astonished.

He glanced again at the beautiful antique furniture

"H.how . . could you have . . come just at the . . right moment?" Eva asked in a very small voice, "and . . s.saved me?"

The Duke took the packed of money which he had collected at the Bank and placed it in her lap.

"I have brought you this from my brother," he said. "It is the £500 he promised to pay you."

"Then . . *Monsieur* Bischoffheim has . . given him . . a cheque."

"Yes, that is right," the Duke replied.

Eva was staring at the packet on her lap which she had not touched.

Then she said: "Please . . will you give it back to Lord Charles? I . . I do not . . want it."

"You certainly earned it," the Duke said.

"I am glad . . I did not make . . any mistakes . . but it is . . unnecessary now . . and I would . . rather not be paid for . . what I did."

The Duke looked puzzled.

Then he said:

"You mean you are rich enough to refuse such a large sum of money, or is there another so-called '*fiance*', in your life?"

"No . . no . . of course . . not!" Eva answered, "but I wanted the money so that I could . . live here in this . . lovely little house . . but now I can go to the *Chateau*."

The Duke stared at her.

"The *Château*? Do you mean where we were last night?"

Eva nodded.

There was silence until the Duke asked:

"Does the *Comte* know that you are a friend of Leonide Leblanc?"

"I told him that I went to her for help because she had been a friend of Papa's . . but he said I was . . not to tell . . anybody . . about her."

"She was a friend of your father's?" the Duke repeated as if he was trying to understand.

Eva gave a little sob.

"Papa . . died in her . . house . . when we were staying here . . and you may think it very wrong . . that I agreed to . . help Lord Charles . . because after I had paid for the . . Funeral there was . . not much . . money left."

Because she was speaking of her father, the tears came into her eyes, and her voice broke.

She felt she must make the Duke understand, and she said:

"I knew if I earned £500 that I could live here for a long time, and pay the servants, but of course, I was lying . . and Mama would have been shocked . . even though . . I was helping . . Lord Charles."

"I am beginning to understand your difficulties," the Duke said in a kind voice, "but I cannot quite understand why the *Comte* has asked you to live with his family."

Eva's eyes flickered, and she looked down before she said:

"I . . I am afraid . . when you met me . . you were told another . . lie about my . . name."

"You mean – it is not Venarde?"

"N.no."

"Then what is your real name?" the Duke asked.

"My father was . . Sir Richard Hillington."

The Duke started.

"Hillington? I cannot believe it!"

"It is true, and we came to . . Paris because Mama had been . . left this lovely house . . by her mother . . who was the *Comtesse* de Chabrillin."

The Duke drew in his breath.

116

"How can you have done anything so foolish as to stay on here alone after your father died, and also to be inveigled into pretending to be my brother's *fiancée*."

Eva did not answer, and the Duke said:

"Surely you should return to England where you must have relations."

"I have a great many," Eva replied, "but I think they never really . . approved of Mama . . any more than the Chabrillins . . approved of Papa when she . . ran away with him."

"I remembered now hearing that your father, whom I have often met on the race-course had caused a great deal of gossip when he was young," the Duke remarked.

"Papa and Mama . . eloped," Eva said, "when she was . . engaged to be married to a . . Frenchman . . whom the Chabrillins had . . chosen for her."

"It was obviously a very brave thing to do," the Duke said.

Eva clasped her hands together.

"Thank you for . . saying that. Mama was very . . very happy with Papa . . although she . . always felt sad that . . her family would not . . speak to her."

"And now you are going to live with them!" the Duke said reflectively, "and you think that will make you happy?"

"They are very, very kind, and I think the *Chateau* is the most beautiful place I have ever seen!"

"I thought the same," the Duke agreed, "except that I prefer my own house."

"Is it very, very impressive?" Eva asked.

"Very!" he replied.

There was the sound of something being knocked over or dropped outside the door. Eva started!

Once again the terror was back in her eyes.

117

"S.someone is . . there!" she said. "You do not . . think . . you do not imagine . . ?"

"Leave it to me," the Duke said.

He rose from the sofa and walked across the room.

Going out of the Salon he shut the door and Eva heard his voice speaking although she could not hear what was said.

The terror of what she had felt with the *Marquis* swept over her and she suddenly felt exhausted.

Once again her hands were shaking.

As she thought about it and she could feel the *Marquis*'s hard lips on her cheek.

She had felt despairingly that if his mouth had taken possession of hers he would have dragged her down into something dirty.

It would be something despicable from which she could not escape.

"I hate him!" she thought.

Then as the Duke did not come back she felt frantic in case he had left her.

If he did so and the *Marquis* returned, she would have no way of protecting herself.

She would be completely at his mercy.

She wanted to run upstairs and lock herself in her bedroom.

Yet it was too difficult to move from the sofa.

She could only lie back against the cushions and close her eyes.

For a moment her head seemed to be swimming, and she felt as if she was sinking into a bottomless pit.

The Duke came back into the room.

He walked to the sofa and looked down at her before he said quietly:

"It is all right! It was only your man-servant. I have

118

given him instructions that nobody is to be allowed into the house."

Eva did not answer and the Duke realised that she was on the verge of collapse.

"Listen to me, Eva," he said gently.

With an effort she opened her eyes.

"What I am going to do," the Duke said, "is to carry you upstairs to bed. I want you to go to sleep and I will fetch you later at eight o'clock, and take you out to dinner."

She gave him a weak smile and he picked her up in his arms.

Carrying her very slowly, he went up the stairs.

When he reached the landing he said:

"You will have to show me which is your bedroom."

Eva did not speak.

She merely made a little gesture with her hand and he managed to open the door.

It was a large room which had obviously been used by her grandmother.

It was as elegantly furnished as the Salon and there were miniatures of the de Chabrillins on each side of the mantelpiece.

There was also a portrait of the *Comtesse* when she had been a girl.

There was a likeness to Eva in the shape and colour of her eyes.

The Duke put Eva gently down on the bed.

Then when he thought it unlikely she would make an effort to undress, he pulled a lace and satin cover over her legs.

"Now, go to sleep," he said, "I will tell your servants to waken you at seven o'clock."

She made a little murmur which he was sure was one of agreement.

119

Then as she lay with her long lashes dark against her pale cheeks he stood for a long time looking down at her.

Only when her breasts moved rhythmically was he aware that she had fallen asleep.

It was a sleep of sheer exhaustion.

He knew that it happened to men after they had been in battle, or in peril on the sea.

They slept dreamlessly from the shock.

The Duke went to the window and pulled the blind half-way down to keep out the sun.

Then with a last look at Eva he went from the room closing the door softly behind him.

He went down the stairs and looked for the servants.

He found Henri and Marie both in the kitchen.

They stood up when he appeared.

He gave them orders clearly and concisely, so that there would be no mistakes.

He then left two golden *louis* on the table and Henri thanked him profusely as he opened the front door.

"*Merci beaucoup, Monsieur, merci!*" he said several times.

"Now, you understand?" the Duke said in excellent French, "No one is to be allowed into the house, except myself."

"*Oui, oui, Monsieur*, your orders will be obeyed," Henri replied.

The Duke stepped into the Chaise that was waiting and drove surprisingly to the *Rue d'Offement*.

He had heard from Eva such a tangled tale that it seemed incredible.

He wanted confirmation of all she had told him.

The one person, he thought, who knew the truth, was Leonide Leblanc.

When he arrived there her man-servant informed him

120

that she had just come home from a luncheon-party and was alone in the Salon.

"Announce me!" the Duke ordered, giving his name.

Leonide was looking, what Eva would have thought, even more theatrical and fantastic than usual.

Her gown was crimson and was obviously a Frederick Worth creation.

The bustle consisted of frill upon frill, ornamented with velvet and lace and a number of silk flowers.

The rows of pearls she wore round her neck were, the Duke thought, worth a 'King's ransom'.

Her ear-rings which matched them had diamond drops the size of olives.

As his name was announced Leonide was obviously surprised.

Then she moved towards him with a grace for which she was famous.

"Is it really Charles's redoubtable brother?" she asked. "I have, *Monsieur*, always longed to meet you."

"The omission can be remedied now," the Duke replied, "for the simple reason that I need your help."

Leonide gave a little exclamation of horror.

"Your brother is not in trouble? Surely, Bischoffheim has paid what he owes?"

"Yes, he has paid," the Duke affirmed.

"Then, please, *Monsieur*, sit down and tell me all about it," Leonide suggested. "I have been worrying in case something should go wrong at the last moment."

The Duke sat down comfortably and crossed his legs.

"I am most gratified to you," he said, "for taking such an interest in Charles and, as I understand, saving him from a situation which might have proved disastrous!"

"I could not imagine, Your Grace, that you would have

121

been very pleased to have Bischoffheim's daughter for your sister-in-law."

"It is something I would have greatly disliked," the Duke said, "and my brother tells me I have to thank you for most cleverly saving him."

"I am glad to have been of service," Leonide said with a provocative smile.

She moved a little nearer to the Duke as she asked:

"And now, what can I do for you?"

"It is quite simple," the Duke said, "I want you to tell me how you met Eva Hillington."

Leonide looked at him as she was trying to read his thoughts.

Then she said perceptively:

"Are you thinking that Charles and Eva have told you lies? It is actually quite simple."

"Then please tell me the truth," the Duke begged.

"Sir Richard Hillington who was an old friend of mine," Leonide said, "inadvertently dropped his shirt – stud when he collapsed with a heart-attack. After he was buried his daughter came to ask me if it was here."

"Her father's shirt-stud?" the Duke repeated beneath his breath. "So that is how you know her!"

"While she was here," Leonide went on, "your brother arrived, having just learnt of Raphael Bischoffheim's intention of making him his son-in-law."

Leonide threw up her hands in an eloquent gesture.

"*Hélas*! From that moment the wheels started turning."

The Duke laughed.

"Of course. That Eva should be Charles's *fiancée* was your Idea. Everybody has always said you are the most intelligent woman in Paris."

"That is what I like to believe," Leonide said, "and now, tell me what has happened to your brother, and of course, to Eva."

"I have sent Charles back to England," the Duke answered, "and he has asked me to give you a present. One of the reasons why I have called is to ask you what I can buy you that you do not already have."

Leonide laughed.

"That is an easy question, when I am asked it by an Englishman."

She looked at the Duke from under her eye-lashes as she spoke, and the Duke asked:

"Well? What is it?"

"What could it be but a horse!" Leonide replied.

The Duke smiled.

"Very well, you shall have one which you will be proud to ride, and I will arrange to send it over as soon as possible."

"*Merci, Monsieur,*" Leonide said, "*vous êtes très gentil.*"

She moved a little nearer still as she spoke, and her lips were raised to his.

"You must thank my brother when you next see him," the Duke said. "It is his present, not mine."

Leonide was too experienced with men not to understand what lay behind his words.

She rose from the sofa.

"Now you must excuse me if I go to lie down," she said. "I have someone calling on me very shortly, and I also have several parties tonight, which will doubtless go on until very late."

The Duke rose.

"Let me thank you again," he said, "and I know, because you are a wise woman, you will not speak of this to anybody."

"I would not do anything which would hurt either your brother, of whom I am very fond, or Eva, whom I have already instructed to tell no one she has ever met me."

"I can only say again – you are a very wise woman!"
He lifted her hand to his lips and said:

"You shall have a horse on which you will look like the 'Queen of Paris' which you undoubtedly are!"

Having left Leonide the Duke drove back to the *Comte's* house.

As soon as he entered the hall he realised that his host had returned.

He walked into the Study to find him alone.

"Hello!" the *Comte* said, "and how is the Emperor?"

"In bad health and depressed," the Duke replied.

"You mean – the Prussians are making more trouble than usual?"

The Duke accepted a glass of champagne which the *Comte* handed to him and sat down in an armchair.

"If you ask me," he said, "the French are running into a trap, and unless they behave more intelligently than they are at the moment, they will challenge the Prussians which will be disastrous."

"I agree with you completely," the *Comte* said, "it would be absolutely disastrous! Did you tell the Emperor so?"

"His Majesty gave me the impression that he is being advised by too many people, at the same time being pushed by the Empress into a confrontation with a nation she has always disliked."

"Women should not interfere in politics, or in national affairs!" the *Comte* averred angrily.

"At the same time," the Duke went on, "there is quite a number of Frenchmen who think they can ride into battle with a flourish of flags and trumpets and win, just because they are French."

"I know exactly what you are saying," the *Comte* replied, "and somebody ought to do something before it is too late."

124

"That is just what I thought myself," the Duke said.

They talked until the *Comte* said he must dress for dinner which was the reason why he had come to Paris.

"I am dining with the Prince Napoleon tonight," he told the Duke. "He has been predicting for years that we are playing into the enemy's hands, but no one will listen to him."

When the Duke went upstairs to dress he was looking very serious.

He knew it had been reported that the Prussians had a large well-trained Army on the borders of France.

The French, with their wild extravagance, fascinating women and endless search for pleasure, would if it came to war, be able to put up very little resistance.

"If the French Army is defeated," the Duke told himself, "the Prussians might even besiege Paris!"

It seemed unlikely.

At the same time the two countries had never been compatible.

While the Duke knew their Statesmen insulted each other both privately and publicly.

As he had his bath the Duke was thinking how much the Prussians would enjoy humiliating the French.

He also knew how agonising it would be for the citizens of Paris.

Then he told himself that it was no use worrying over other people's affairs.

Thank God, the British had always had the Channel between them and the Continent.

When he dressed he found his host had already left the house.

But one of the *Comte*'s comfortable carriages was waiting for him.

He drove towards the *Rue St. Honore*, aware that he was looking forward to seeing Eva again.

She was undoubtedly extremely lovely in a very original and unusual manner.

Now he could understand her fair hair with its touched of gold came, like her fair skin, from her father.

It was her mother who had provided her dark eyes.

He had seen her exquisite features in the *Comte*'s children when he had been at the *Château*.

He thought it very remiss that he had not realised then that there was a distinct resemblance between Eva and the *Comte*'s youngest daughter, who was seventeen.

But Eva also had a vibrant personality of which he had been aware from the moment he had first met her.

What he had not been able to understand was that she was frightened of him.

He had thought at first that it was because he had not been told of her engagement to Charles.

She had continued to avoid him and had even run away from him when he had sought her out in the Library.

Then he had known that it was something deeper.

It was fear, he knew now.

A fear which was something sensitive and very different from the terror the *Marquis* had aroused in her.

He knew that even as Eva had struggled with him, she had not fully understood exactly what the Frenchman intended.

The Duke thought that only by the grace of God had he arrived in time.

He had been able to save her from an experience which would have scarred her for life.

When he had carried her up the stairs he had thought how fragile she was.

She had been very light in his arms.

When he put her down on the bed she looked like

a Fairy Princess who had fallen asleep for a hundred years.

Then he remembered the tale of the Sleeping Beauty – awakened with a kiss from a Prince.

He knew as he had stood there looking down at her that he had wanted to kiss Eva.

Even if only to reassure her that she need not be afraid.

He was quite certain after what Charles had said that she had never been kissed.

It was extremely regrettable that her first experience of a man who desired her should have been with the *Marquis*. He was a dissolute and somewhat debauched man.

The Duke knew a great deal about him that he had no intention of telling Eva.

He was thinking that she would have to protect herself from him and a great number of men like him.

When she had done so she would lose her elusive innocent charm.

It made her different from the women with whom he usually came in contact.

"I must talk to her about the future," he told himself firmly.

He stepped from the carriage to where Henri was holding open the front door.

He was looking forward to the evening with a very strange feeling in his heart.

. . . .

Eva was waiting for the Duke in the Salon.

As Henri showed him in he saw her jump up from the chair in which she had been sitting.

She took a step forward as if she wanted to run towards him.

127

Then as if she checked herself, she walked slowly until they met in the centre of the room.

She dropped him a curtsy.

She was looking, he realised, very lovely.

He was not aware that once again she was wearing one of her mother's gowns.

It was one which Josie had admired and said needed nothing to make it more perfect.

She had taken it with her to the *Château* in case they had stayed a second night.

But now it made her look smart enough for a much more important occasion than the quiet Restaurant to which he was taking her.

"Are you feeling better?" the Duke asked.

She looked up at him with shining eyes and said:

"I slept until Marie woke me and now I must apologise for behaving so . . stupidly."

"You were not stupid and it was understandable in the circumstances," he replied.

He saw the pleasure in her eyes. Then she said in a different tone:

"I . . I have something to . . ask you."

"What is it?" he asked.

"It was . . very kind of you to . . escort me out to dinner . . but perhaps it is . . incorrect to be alone with you . . and my Uncle might be . . angry with me."

The Duke smiled.

"It is certainly something which would not be allowed if you were staying at the *Château* with the *Comtesse*. But as you have not yet taken up residence there they have for the moment no jurisdiction over you."

"So I may come with . . you," Eva asked eagerly.

"I shall be very disappointed if you refuse, and we are going somewhere which is very quiet where no one will see us, and no one will gossip about us tomorrow."

128

"Then that will be lovely!" Eva said. "Papa took me to two Restaurants in Paris when we first arrived, and I was afraid now that I would never be able to go to one again."

"We are going to one where the food is famous," the Duke said, "and I shall be disappointed if you do not enjoy it."

"I shall enjoy every moment," Eva promised.

"Then what are we waiting for?" he asked.

She smiled at him and he thought she seemed almost to float over the floor until they reached the hall.

There was a velvet wrap to put over her shoulders.

When they stepped into the carriage, Eva said:

"This is very exciting for me, but I am sure, because you are so important, that you should be taking somebody out like . . "

She stopped.

The Duke knew she had been about to say "Leonide Leblanc" then realised she had been told not to mention her.

Instead Eva said a little lamely:

" . . the lovely ladies who I have seen in the *Bois*."

"If you are looking for compliments," the Duke said, "I can assure you Eva, you are as lovely in fact, lovelier than any lady I have seen in the *Bois* since I arrived."

Eva gave a little cry of delight.

He thought it was very child-like and very touching

"I want to believe you," she said, "because nobody has . . ever said . . anything like . . that to me . . before."

"Then I am privileged to be the first," the Duke replied.

They drove to the *Rue Madeleine*.

There was a Restaurant near the Church where the Duke often dined when he was in Paris.

It was not fashionable, but the food was outstanding and "*Larue*" was patronised by epicures.

There was a table in an alcove which he knew of old was where one could dine and see but not be seen.

He could tell from the expression on Eva's face as they sat down that she was thrilled with her surroundings

There were comfortable sofa-seats and lighted candles on the tables.

Flowers were very much part of the decor and there was no music.

Eva looked around.

Then as she took off her gloves she said in a very young, excited voice:

"It is . . very thrilling to be here . . with you!"

She looked at the Duke as she spoke, and as their eyes met, it was difficult to look away.

CHAPTER SEVEN

The Duke took a long time choosing the food and the wine.

When the waiters had left them he sat back in his chair and said:

"I would be very remiss if I did not tell you that you look lovely!"

Eva blushed.

He thought it was something he had not seen a woman do for a long time.

When the food came it was delicious, and Eva knew her father would have appreciated it.

There were also wines with each course of which she took a tiny sip, but left the rest to the Duke.

Only when they were drinking coffee and the Duke had a liqueur beside him did Eva say:

"I shall always remember this dinner and this lovely place to which you brought me."

She spoke in the same rapt little voice he had heard when she saw something beautiful in the *Château*.

He knew it was completely sincere, and came from her heart.

"I would like you to remember it," he said, "and now Eva, I want to talk to you about yourself."

She looked at him apprehensively.

There was silence as she thought he was choosing his words with care.

Then he said:

"Are you quite certain you are wise in being determined to live in France rather than England?"

"I . . I am sure I would be happy at the *Château* where Mama was a girl," Eva replied.

She looked at the Duke, and she had the idea he was worried.

After a moment he said:

"I feel it is a mistake, as your father was English, for you to live in France."

"Why?" Eva asked.

"Well, two things worry me."

"What are they?"

"The first is that I am quite sure that within a year's time there will be a confrontation between France and Germany."

"Do you mean War?" Eva asked in astonishment.

"I am afraid it is inevitable," the Duke replied.

"I cannot believe it!" Eva cried. "Everybody in France seems so happy! Why should they want to fight the Germans?"

"It is a long story," the Duke said, "but I was with the Emperor today, and I was sure he was being pushed into War by the Empress and the *Duc* de Gramont."

"I have heard Papa talk about it," Eva said, "but I cannot believe they would sacrifice so much when everything here seems so delightful and so luxurious."

"The pleasures of Paris!" the Duke said beneath his breath.

He was thinking as he spoke of the wild extravagance of the Courtesans like Leonide Leblanc, and the vast amount of money that men expended on her.

Eva was looking at him anxiously and he said:

132

"If there is a War, which will be between the Prussian Army and the French, who are definitely not so well-equipped, I only hope that you are in a safe place."

"A safe place?" Eva questioned. "But I would be in my Uncle's *Châlteau*."

"Which is less than twenty-five miles outside Paris," the Duke said.

There was silence, then Eva asked:

"Are you suggesting that the Prussians might advance on Paris and capture it?"

"I think," the Duke answered, "it might be besieged."

"I cannot believe it!" Eva whispered.

The Duke had a sip of brandy before he said:

"There is something else I think you have not considered in your decision to stay here."

"What is . . that?"

"It is that your Uncle, being French, would feel it his duty to arrange your marriage."

Eva sat upright in her chair.

"Do you mean," she asked, "that I would have an . . arranged marriage like the one . . mama ran . . away from?"

"Your Uncle would believe it was in your best interests," the Duke said quietly. "As you are well aware, the whole family disapproved of your mother because she married the man she loved."

Eva clasped her hands together.

"I never . . thought of . . that. It was . . foolish of me not to . . remember it."

"She gave a deep sigh.

"You are right . . I must go . . back to England."

"That is what I hoped you would say," the Duke replied. "And I know it is something you will not regret."

Almost beneath her breath Eva said:

133

"Papa's relatives are mostly . . very old . . and they will . . talk and talk . . about him. I feel I could not . . bear that at . . the moment."

"I can understand what you are feeling," the Duke said, "and if you leave it to me, I will find somebody with whom you can stay when you first arrive . . and who will be happy to have you until you find somewhere you really want to live."

"Could you . . do that?" Eva asked. "It would be very . . very kind . . but I would not wish to . . impose on . . you."

"I assure you, you would not be doing that," the Duke said, "and now, because you have had a long and upsetting day, I am going to take you home."

He saw an expression of disappointment on Eva's face and added:

"I am staying in Paris until the day after tomorrow. Have luncheon with your Uncle and tell him you have changed your mind. Then perhaps you would honour me by again being my guest at dinner."

"Of course," Eva exclaimed. "That will be . . wonderful for . . me!"

Her eyes, which had been clouded, were shining again, and the Duke went on:

"The following day, I will take you back to England. And until I do you must not do anything so foolish as walking about the streets alone."

Eva remembered that, when she had walked to visit Leonide Leblanc, the Marquis had seen her.

She gave a little shudder, and the Duke knew what she was thinking.

"Forget him!" he said.

"I . . I will try to," Eva answered, "but when you told me that my Uncle would . . arrange my marriage . . I thought I might have to . . marry . . somebody . . like the Marquis!"

134

"All Frenchmen are not so unpleasant," the Duke said, "and you must remember he was not treating you as if you were your father's daughter."

His voice deepened, and it was almost stern as he added:

"It is always a mistake to lie."

"I . . I know that," Eva agreed humbly, "and Mama . . would have been . . ashamed of me!"

The Duke called for the bill and they left the Restaurant.

Outside the carriage was waiting and it was only a short way to the *Rue St. Honoré*.

Eva did not speak.

The Duke, looking at her profile silhouetted against the window by the lights outside, thought she was very beautiful.

'How can she possibly look after herself?' he asked, 'when every men who sees her finds her irresistible!'

It was his experience which told him it was not only because she was so lovely that men would desire her.

There was an aura of innocence and purity about her which Leonide Leblanc had recognised.

While men like the Marquis would instinctively desire her.

The horses drew up outside the little house and as they came to a standstill Eva said in a very small, frightened voice:

"Suppose . . just suppose that . . while I have . . been away . . he has got into the . . house?"

The Duke was aware that the terror was back in her eyes and her hands were shaking.

"I will make quite certain he has not," he said gently.

He told the carriage to wait.

When Henri opened the door he walked into the house beside Eva.

They went into the Salon where there were still some candles alight in the candelabra.

As they did so they heard Henri close the front door and shuffle back to the kitchen.

Eva looked up at the Duke as if she was waiting for him to take the initiative.

He smiled at her, put out his hand and took hers.

"Now, we are going to explore the house together," he said, "then you can sleep without being frightened of anything."

She gave him a shy little smile.

As if she was a child, he took her first round the Salon.

He looked behind the curtains and an attractive screen which stood in one corner of the room.

Then they walked across the empty hall to the Dining-Room.

Small and very attractive, it had an oval table and a marble mantelpiece which the Duke recognised as being 17th Century.

Again he checked the curtains and even looked under the table.

They walked up the stairs to the First Floor.

Here it was much darker and the only light came from the candles in the sconces below them in the hall.

The Duke felt Eva's fingers tighten on his.

He went to the first door which was her bedroom, and opened it.

As he did so there was a crash.

Eva gave a scream and flung herself against him holding on to him frantically.

He put his arms around her.

In the light of one candle by the bed he saw that

the crash had been caused by the draught from the window.

This had caused the curtain to billow out and knock down a plant that was on a table nearby.

It was still billowing out, but he was quite certain there was nobody behind it.

At the same time, Eva was so terrified and he could feel her whole body shaking.

"It is all right," the Duke said soothingly.

"It is him . . it is . . him!" Eva murmured. "Save me . . save me again."

She looked up at him pleadingly.

The Duke knew he had never known anyone so frightened.

"I will save you, my darling," he said.

As he spoke he pulled her closer still and his lips were on hers.

For a moment Eva could hardly believe it was happening.

Then as the Duke took possession of her lips she knew her fear had left her.

Instead, something incredibly wonderful was happening.

At first, the Duke's kiss was very gentle, as if he was afraid to frighten her more than she was already.

Then as he felt the softness and innocence of her lips, his lips became more demanding, more insistent.

It was to Eva as if the Heavens had opened. She had been carried up on a shaft of moonlight and was among the stars.

The moonlight seemed to be seeping through her body.

It was moving with an indescribable ecstasy through her breasts and on to her lips.

When the Duke raised his head she made a little murmur because she was losing him.

At the same time, the wonder of it was so overwhelming that she could only hide her face against his shoulder.

"You are quite, quite safe now, my precious," he said, in a voice that sounded a little unsteady, "and I will never let anyone hurt you!"

"I . . I love . . you," Eva whispered.

Once again there was that rapt note in her voice.

When she looked at him he knew there was a spiritual ecstasy in her face which he had never seen before.

"And I love you," he said, "and I have done for a long time."

"For a . . long . . time?"

"Ever since I first saw you, but I thought you belonged to my brother."

"And I . . thought you . . disapproved of . . me," Eva whispered.

"I disapproved of you marrying Charles because I wanted you for myself!"

His arms tightened.

"How could you have tortured me, my darling, by letting me think you would be my sister-in-law, when I wanted you as my wife?"

Eva gave a little cry and it seemed like the song of the angels.

Then she said in a whisper the Duke could hardly hear:

"Are you . . are you . . asking me to . . marry you?"

The Duke smiled.

"How else can I look after you and protect you? You are far too beautiful to be left alone for a moment!"

"I love you . . I love you with . . all of me! But . . I did not understand it was . . love."

138

"I will teach you about love," the Duke said, "and if any other man attempts to do so – I will kill him!"

Eva looked at him adoringly, and he went on:

"I did not mean to tell you about my love until we knew each other better, and I had taken you back to England."

"Now I . . understand why you . . wanted me to . . return home," Eva said.

"That was the principal reason. At the same time, the two objections I gave you about the War and being a French citizen are very valid."

"I want . . to be English . . and I . . want to be . . with you!" Eva said passionately.

"That is what you will be," the Duke promised, "and if, my darling, you love me enough, we can be married before we return to England."

"I love you . . so much that I . . want to . . marry you now . . at once . . at this . . moment!" Eva said.

The Duke laughed.

"That would be rather difficult, but I will try to arrange it for tomorrow, or perhaps the day after."

Eva put her head against his shoulder.

"You . . are quite . . quite certain you . . want to marry me?"

"I have never wanted to marry anyone before," the Duke said. "In fact, everybody believes I am a confirmed bachelor."

There was silence. Then Eva said:

"Supposing . . when you . . have married me . . you are disappointed . . and think you have . . made a mistake?"

The Duke smiled.

"You are everything I have ever wanted in my wife, and I love and adore everything about you. I also want to know a great deal more."

139

Eva looked at him solemnly.

"Will you promise to . . teach me to do . . all the things you want me to do?"

"I promise," the Duke said, "but I want you to be just as you are, and your real self."

Eva hid her face against him.

"I am . . so ashamed now that I . . lied."

The Duke knew it was not because she had lied that she had run into trouble.

It was because she had become involved with Leonide Leblanc.

At the same time, if she had not gone to see her to find her father's shirt-stud, he would never have met her.

"Fate moves in mysterious ways, my precious one," he said, "and all we have to remember is that we have found each other, and in the future we will be very, very happy."

"You do not . . think," Eva asked, "that it will be . . a shock to your family that you have . . married somebody . . as unimportant as . . me?"

"I think quite a number of them will have met your father," he said, "in which case, he would have charmed them as he charmed everybody he met."

"That is what I . . like to . . hear you . . say," Eva said, "and perhaps . . I shall be able to . . charm them too."

"I am quite certain you will," the Duke said, "just as you have charmed me."

He kissed her again and went on kissing her.

Now she was travelling on a rainbow into a Heaven she had never known existed.

"It is a heaven of Love," she told herself.

She felt such an indescribable ecstasy that she thought no one could feel such sensations and not die of the wonder of it.

140

Finally the Duke said:

"I want to stay here, my darling, kissing you and telling you how wonderful you are, but you must go to sleep."

Because she felt so happy, Eva had forgotten her fear that the *Marquis* might be hiding somewhere.

Then as she glanced across the room the Duke said:

"We will just finish exploring the house. Light some candles while I shut the windows."

Eva did as he told her and the extra candles made the room seem warm and glamorous.

The Duke shut the window but before he did so he looked outside.

There was a sheer drop to the small garden.

It was impossible for anybody to climb up, unless they had a very long ladder.

He did not say anything, but pulled the curtains to, and picked up the plant which was lying on the floor.

Then he walked across the room, and taking Eva by the hand as he had before, he took her out into the passage.

They explored the other two bedrooms which were rather smaller than the one in which Eva was sleeping.

There was no one in them.

As they came out the Duke locked the doors on the outside and gave Eva the keys.

"Now you are to lock yourself in," he said, "and I will tell your man-servant that no one – and I mean no one – is to be allowed to enter the house until I arrive tomorrow morning."

"You will not . . forget me?"

"That would be impossible."

The Duke was standing at the top of the stairs and he held her close against him.

Then he said:

"To make things easier for you, my lovely one, I am going to tell your Uncle, whom I shall see at breakfast tomorrow morning, that we are to be married."

He paused to look at her tenderly.

"There will be no point therefore in you having luncheon with him as he had arranged."

"You will tell him I am very . . grateful for his . . kindness?" Eva said.

"Of course I will," the Duke agreed, "but as I want to be with you every minute, we will have luncheon quietly. By that time I shall have a lot to tell you as to when and how we can be married."

Eva gave a little murmur of joy.

Then he was kissing her gently and very lovingly, as if she was infinitely precious.

"Now go into your bedroom," he said, "and let me hear you lock the door, and try to go to sleep."

"I shall say my . . prayers and thank God a . . million times that you . . love me," Eva said.

As if her words moved him, the Duke kissed her forehead.

Then he turned her round to push her gently through the door of her bedroom and shut it behind her.

He heard her turn the key in the lock, then he went downstairs.

He gave his orders to Henri, tipped him because he had stayed up late.

Then he heard the bolts on the front door go into place before he drove away.

His carriage carried him back to the house near the *Bois*.

He knew he was prepared to dedicate his whole life to loving and protecting Eva.

He had never felt like this about any other woman.

He knew how utterly helpless she was without him.

There were terrible difficulties in which she could find herself, not only in France but also in England.

"She needs me," he told himself, "and she is what I need, but never realised it until now."

. . . .

When the Duke came down to breakfast, the *Comte* was already sitting at the table with the Newspaper open in front of him.

"The papers are already working the public up against the Prussians," he said. "I can only hope they will not go too far."

The Duke did not reply.

He had already told the *Comte* his feelings as to what would happen, and knew he had not been believed.

Instead he changed the subject.

He told the *Comte* that he was going to marry Eva.

The *Comte* was completely astonished.

"I had no idea! It never struck me for a moment that you were interested in her," he said.

The Duke smiled.

"I find her completely adorable."

"I agree with you, but of course, I am delighted for one of my most distinguished friends to marry my niece."

"I hoped that was how you would feel," the Duke said, "and now I want your help."

It was the *Comte* as the Duke hoped, who made everything easy for him and Eva to have a secret marriage.

"If the British Embassy get to hear of it," he said, "it will be blazoned over every newspaper in England!"

"That is what I thought," the Duke agreed. "In which case, as you are aware, Eva will be criticized for marrying when she is in deep mourning, and there will be a great many speculations as to why the marriage should take place so quickly."

143

The two men did not need to say any more to each other.

Both were aware of how unpleasant gossip could be.

The Duke and the *Comte* had worked out what they thought was a perfect plan.

Then the Duke borrowed one of the *Comte* Phaetons and drove to Eva's house in the *Rue St. Honoré*.

She was dressed in one of her prettiest gowns, and was waiting for him in the Salon.

As he came into the room and Henri shut the door behind him she took a little step towards him.

Then she hesitated although she was longing to run to his side.

He smiled and held out his arms and the next minute she was in them.

He could feel her whole body quivering with excitement.

He kissed her until they were both breathless.

Then he said:

"Let me look at you, my darling. Did you sleep well?"

"I slept . . and I dreamt you were . . kissing me."

"That is what I was dreaming too," the Duke replied.

He kissed her again, then drew her towards the sofa.

"I have so much to tell you," he said.

"Which I am longing to hear," Eva replied quickly.

"First," the Duke began, "tell me you have not changed your mind."

Eva laughed, and it was a very pretty sound.

"I was afraid . . you might have . . changed yours."

"That would be impossible," the Duke said.

She lifted her lips to his, but he pushed her a little away from him.

"You are not to tempt me," he said. "I want to kiss you, and go on kissing you, but first you have to listen to what I have planned."

144

"You are not . . sending me . . back to England . . without you?"

"Do you really think I would do such a thing?"

"I was only . . afraid you . . would think that . . the right thing to do."

"What we are going to do," he explained, "are all the things which other people might think were wrong, but everything that is right for us."

Eva clasped her hands together and moved a little closer to him.

"We are . . going to be . . married?" she whispered.

"A secret marriage which no one will know about for a long time."

"Tell me . . please . . tell me."

"I have worked it out with your Uncle," the Duke said, "who, incidentally is delighted that you are marrying me."

"You are . . quite sure he is . . not angry?"

"Not in the least," the Duke smiled. "He is very pleased to have an English Duke in the family."

Eva laughed.

"What we have arranged," the Duke went on, "is that your Uncle is at the moment having our marriage registered at the *Mairie* so that in an hour's time, you will legally be my wife."

Eva drew in her breath and her eyes seemed to fill her face.

She did not speak, and the Duke went on:

"Because your Uncle has influence, the Mayor will not make the announcement public and everything will be kept secret until we are ready to send a notice of our marriage to the English newspapers."

Eva made a little murmur of excitement, and the Duke continued:

"This evening at six o'clock your Uncle will call for

145

you and take you to the house of one of his friends, who has his own private Chapel."

Eva slipped her hand into the Duke's as if she wanted to hold onto him and he said:

"We will be married by a Priest who is your Uncle's private Chaplain, who will of course never reveal what has occurred."

Eva looked up at him with a puzzled expression in her eyes.

"A . . Priest?" she questioned.

"It was your Uncle who told me that after you were born your mother wrote to her mother, your grandmother and told her that because she had been brought up a Catholic you had been baptised into the Catholic Faith. Then because she loved your father also as a Protestant."

Eva gave a little cry.

"Now you mention it, I remember Mama telling me that a long time ago. I never thought of it again because Mama and Papa always went to an English Church near our home."

She paused before she said:

"Mama loved him so much that she always did exactly what he wished . . and never thought of . . herself."

"Will you do the same?" the Duke asked.

"I will . . always do what you want . . as Mama once said . . love is more important than . . anything else."

"Of course it is!" the Duke agreed, "and the love we have for each other, my beautiful little wife-to-be, comes from God and is greater than any Service or ritual. I believe in all truth, it is part of the Divine."

He spoke very solemnly, and Eva said:

"How can you . . think as I think . . believe as I do? I never thought I would find a man . . who could do that."

"Now you have found me," the Duke said, "and after we are married we will be one person."

"It will be . . wonderful to be a part of you," Eva said, "and I shall always . . remember that you are the . . most important part!"

The Duke smiled.

"That, of course, is what I want you to think, but nothing in the world is more important to me than you!"

He kissed her again and she knew that no one could be more wonderful.

They had a quiet luncheon together, talking about themselves.

When Eva went back to her house she told Henri and Marie she was going to be married.

They were extremely excited and impressed, and promised to keep it a complete secret.

"My husband and I will be staying here tonight," Eva went on, "but tomorrow we are leaving for Venice. After that we are going to Rome and Naples where we will take a yacht which my husband will charter and visit the many places in the Mediterranean."

As she spoke she thought that nothing could be more exciting than to be alone with the Duke.

She also wanted to see all the places about which she had read, but thought she would never have the opportunity of visiting.

But all that really mattered, she thought, was to be with him.

"We are going to have a very long honeymoon, my precious," the Duke had said, "and only just before we return to England will our marriage be announced, without the actual date when it took place. If people assume it was a week or so before then, that is their business and now ours."

He smiled at her.

"Then you will be able to go back home without wearing mourning, so there will be no one saying that you should have waited until after your father's death for a longer time before you took a husband."

"I know Papa would . . want me to marry . . you and would . . think like . . that," Eva said.

"I am sure he would," the Duke replied, "and I know your father would want me to look after you."

"Now I shall feel safe for ever . . and ever!" Eva said, "and I need . . never be . . afraid again!"

"Never!" the Duke agreed firmly.

. . . .

When the Duke left her in her house, on his instructions she promised Henri and Marie that she would increase their wages.

They were to look after everything for her and she would come to Paris as often as she could.

As she was going upstairs wondering what gown she should wear in which to be married, a box was delivered at the door.

It contained a very beautiful wedding-gown from Frederick Worth.

It was so exquisite that Eva could not believe it was really for her.

When she put it on Marie admitted that the Duke had taken one of her gowns away with him.

That was how he knew the exact size of her tiny waist.

The bustle in silver tulle ornamented with diamanté made the gown so beautiful that Eva was almost afraid to wear it.

When she was dressed there was a veil over her hair held down by a wreath of orange blossom.

As she looked in the mirror she knew that all she wanted was for the Duke to admire her.

148

She knew too that although it would be a small and quiet Service it would be something neither of them would ever forget.

She drove with her Uncle to a huge mansion in the *Champs Elysees*.

When she saw the Duke waiting for her in the tiny Chapel, her heart turned a thousand somersaults.

In evening dress, wearing his decorations as was correct in France, the Duke looked handsome yet at the same time very English.

Her Uncle took her up the sort aisle on his arm.

Then as the Duke took her hand in his the Service began.

It was very short because, although Eva was counted as a Catholic, the Duke was a Protestant.

The Priest said the words in Latin and in French so that they both understood.

When they knelt for the blessing, Eva knew she had indeed been blessed.

She would thank God all her life for letting her find the Duke.

Because he knew it would please the *Comte* the Duke had agreed that they would go back to his house.

There they drank champagne.

The *Comte* said over and over again how pleased he was that his niece was now the Duchess of Kincraig.

"I had intended to find you a husband, my dear," he said to Eva, "but even if I had searched the whole of France I doubt if I could have found you a man more distinguished or more charming . . "

Eva drew in her breath and slipped her hand into her husband's.

She knew he was thinking he had been right in saying that the *Comte* would have considered it his duty to marry her to some aristocrat.

She had been saved from that.

Before they drove away back to the little house, that was waiting for them the *Comte* gave Eva a present.

It was a very beautiful brooch from Oscar Masin a famous Jeweller who had made many lovely things for the Empress.

The Duke knew he had also created some magnificent pieces of jewellery for the Courtesans.

He waited until they were back in the *Rue St. Honore* before he said:

"You have had one wedding present, my darling, and now I want to give you mine."

"But . . I have . . nothing for . . you!" Eva cried.

"You can give me a present which I want more than anything else in the world," the Duke replied, "but I will tell you about that later."

She was not quite certain what he meant.

At the same time, because of the way he spoke she blushed.

He kissed her before he said:

"There are wonderful jewels waiting for you at Castle Kincraig when we arrive home, but this is something very special which is all your own, and which I hope you will always wear."

As he spoke he brought from his coat-tails a velvet box.

He opened it and Eva saw a most exquisite ring made in the shape of a heart.

In the centre was a diamond surrounded by diamonds.

As they glittered in the light, she knew it was the most precious thing she had ever owned.

She kissed her husband and he held her so close that it was difficult to breathe.

"There are thousands more things I want to give you,"

he said, "but we will have time on our honeymoon to search for treasures and they will always remind us of our happiness."

"Then they will be very, very precious!" Eva said quietly.

The Duke had arranged for dinner to be sent from '*Larue*' where they had dined the precious night.

Henri, helped by a young waiter, served it with a flourish.

They were all dishes, Eva knew, that the Duke had discovered she liked the best.

But it was difficult to think of what she was eating, and she kept thinking how handsome he was.

She knew by the expression in his eyes that he was thinking only of her.

There were sudden silences in what they were saying, and they spoke to each other without words.

. . . .

It was much later that night in the bed which Eva had always felt was too big for one small person.

She moved against the Duke's shoulder and he asked:

"Are you awake, my lovely one?"

"How can I . . ever sleep again . . when I am . . so happy?" Eva asked.

"I have made you happy?"

"So wildly, ecstatically happy that I cannot believe I am . . still alive . . or if I am . . I must be dreaming!"

"You are very much alive," the Duke said, "and darling, we will go on dreaming for a very long time."

Eva pressed her cheek against him.

"Y.you were . . not disappointed in me?" she whispered.

"How can you think anything so foolish?" he answered, "you were perfect and my precious, no man could have a more enchanting wedding present."

"Do you . . mean . . me?" Eva asked.

"Yes, my beautiful wife, I mean you!"

"I . . did not know that . . love could be so . . wonderful," Eva said. "I . . I did not understand . . that it could be even more marvellous than your . . kisses!"

"Is that what it was?" the Duke enquired.

"There are . . no words to tell you that when you . . loved me you took me into Heaven . . and I think I am . . still there!"

"That is where we will always be," the Duke said, "in our own special secret Heaven, my precious heart, where nobody will ever frighten you."

"I . . love . . you! I . . love you!" Eva murmured.

It was something they both said to each other a hundred times.

But there was no other way in which they could express the glory and ecstasy of their love.

It came from Heaven, it was part of Heaven and would be theirs for Eternity.

Other books by Barbara Cartland

Romantic Novels, over 400, the most recently published being:

The Perfect Pearl	A Revolution of Love
Love is a Maze	The Marquis Wins
A Circus for Love	Love is the Key
The Temple of Love	Free as the Wind
The Bargain Bride	Desire in the Desert
The Haunted Heart	A Heart in the Highlands
Real Love or Fake	The Music of Love
A Kiss from a Stranger	The Wrong Duchess
A Very Special Love	The Taming of a Tigress
A Necklace of Love	Love Comes to the Castle

The Dream and the Glory (In aid of the St. John Ambulance Brigade)

Autobiographical and Biographical:

The Isthmus Years 1919–1939
The Years of Opportunity 1939–1945
I Search for Rainbows 1945–1976
We Danced All Night 1919–1929
Ronald Cartland (With a foreword by Sir Winston Churchill)
Polly – My Wonderful Mother
I Seek the Miraculous

Historical:

Bewitching Women
The Outrageous Queen (The Story of Queen Christina of Sweden)
The Scandalous Life of King Carol
The Private Life of Charles II
The Private Life of Elizabeth, Empress of Austria
Josephine, Empress of France
Diane de Poitiers
Metternich – The Passionate Diplomat
A Year of Royal Days
Royal Lovers
Royal Jewels
Royal Eccentrics

Sociology:

You in the Home
The Fascinating Forties
Marriage for Moderns
Be Vivid, Be Vital
Love, Life and Sex
Vitamins for Vitality
Husbands and Wives
Men are Wonderful

Etiquette
The Many Facets of Love
Sex and the Teenager
The Book of Charm
Living Together
The Youth Secret
The Magic of Honey
The Book of Beauty and Health

Keep Young and Beautiful by Barbara Cartland and Elinor Glyn
Etiquette for Love and Romance
Barbara Cartland's Book of Health

General:

Barbara Cartland's Book of Useless Information with a Foreword by the
    Earl Mountbatten of Burma.
   (In aid of the United World Colleges)
Love and Lovers (Picture Book)
The Light of Love (Prayer Book)
Barbara Cartland's Scrapbook
(In aid of the Royal Photographic Museum)
Romantic Royal Marriages
Barbara Cartland's Book of Celebrities
Getting Older, Growing Younger

Verse:

Lines on Life and Love

Music:

An Album of Love Songs
sung with the Royal Philharmonic Orchestra.

Films:

A Hazard of Hearts
The Lady and the Highwayman
A Ghost in Monte Carlo
A Duel of Love

Cartoons:

Barbara Cartland Romances (Book of Cartoons)
has recently been published in the U.S.A., Great Britain,
and other parts of the world.

Children:

A Children's Pop-Up Book: "Princess to the Rescue"

Cookery:

Barbara Cartland's Health Food Cookery Book
Food for Love
Magic of Honey Cookbook
Recipes for Lovers
The Romance of Food

Editor of:

"The Common Problem" by Ronald Cartland (with a preface by the Rt.
Hon. the Earl of Selborne, P.C.)
Barbara Cartland's Library of Love
Library of Ancient Wisdom
"Written with Love" Passionate love letters selected by Barbara
Cartland

Drama:

Blood Money
French Dressing

Philosophy:

Touch the Stars

Radio Operetta:

The Rose and the Violet
(Music by Mark Lubbock) Performed in 1942.

Radio Plays:

The Caged Bird: An episode in the life of Elizabeth Empress of Austria.
Performed in 1957.

Magic From the Heart

Unexpectedly summoned home from Florence, Lady Safina Wick has no inkling of the bombshell that awaits her at Dover. She is to be forced into marrying a man she has never seen — the impoverished Duke of Dallwyn. But more surprising still is the power with which the Duke and Safina confront their situation — a deep and magical love.

Too Precious to Lose

Lord Sedgewyn's beautiful daughter always suspected her stepmother hated her. But she never could have known quite how much until her supper poisoned the kitchen cat. Fleeing for her life, Norina finds thin ice for safety when she meets another, more mysterious, fugitive — the blind but handsome *Marquis* de Chalamont.